Dream

Challenge

Best,

Titles by Gregory S Smith

Dream Challenge

CIO 2.0

Straight to the Top: CIO Leadership in a Mobile, Social, and Cloud-based World

Protecting Your Children on the Internet: A Road Map for Parents and Teachers

How to Protect Your Children on the Internet: A Road Map for Parents and Teachers

Straight to the Top: Becoming a World-Class CIO

Mr. Smith's books are for sale around the world in print and e-book. They have been translated into multiple languages, including most recently, Mandarin and Portuguese.

Dream Challenge

A Fiction Thriller by

Gregory S Smith

This book is a work of fiction. Names, characters, places, dreams, and incidents are the product of the author's imagination or are used fictitiously. Any resemblance to actual events, locales, or persons, living or dead, is purely coincidental.

Copyright © 2017 Gregory S Smith.

First Edition: December 2017

ISBN: 978-0692253182

Printed in the United States of America

10 9 8 7 6 5 4 3 2 1

DEDICATION

To my grandfather and grandmother
– Peter and Angelina Carino.

Your influence helped me become the
business executive, author, professor,
father, and storyteller I am today.

And to my parents – Carl and
Josephine. You always have my back.
Love you!

ACKNOWLEDGMENTS

I'd like to thank my son Danny for his creative ideas towards several of the dream challenges.

I'd also like to thank AJ for her editorial support during this really cool project. Her insights and edits helped me immensely.

Also, thank you Ginger for her insightful recommendations on editorial work. You don't miss!

Finally, I would like to thank my wife Susanna, daughter Anna Kate, son Daniel, and son-in-law Douglas. Thank you for your support of my literary dreams.

A dreamer is one who can only find his way by moonlight, and his punishment is that he sees the dawn before the rest of the world.

- Oscar Wilde

Denial is the first impulse of a traitor.

- Joseph Stalin

Dream Challenge

1 - THE ICE MONKEYS

Tony Blackwell stood in the middle of a room with two other young adults, one man and a woman. He wore a pair of Levi's jeans, one of his favorite Boston Red Sox tee shirts, and a pair of black Nike sneakers. Everyone else in the room was sitting at their chairs and busy writing on notepads that resembled college essay test booklets. The room was painted solid white, floor to ceiling, and set with titanium steel metal tables and chairs. Across the hallway, another man sat in a small room at a table alone, not writing, just sitting alone and staring at the wall.

The stranger sensed that he was being watched, turned his head, raised his eyebrows, and provided Tony with a steely glare.

I wonder what that guy did? thought Tony. "Damn, what am I doing here?" Tony said softly as he turned his head to disengage the stranger's glance.

"Have a seat Mr. Blackwell," said a tall man hovering in the center of the room who appeared out of thin air. Before Tony could get his question out, the man answered almost instinctively. "I am Mr. Y and I'm your host," he continued.

"Host of what?" replied Tony.

"Please sit. I'll explain all of the rules in a moment," replied Mr. Y as he gestured toward the open chair. Tony quietly took a seat and looked around the table at the others. As Tony made eye contact with them, they all looked away, mostly down at their notepads.

"What are we doing here? What rules?" questioned Tony. Mr. Y was dressed in a full-length white robe, adorned with a golden twisted rope tied around his waist. *He doesn't have any feet,* thought Tony. *Why can't I see his feet?* Mr. Y resembled an ancient prophet or holy man, and appeared to float as he moved across the room. His pure white robe dusted across the pristine white tiled floor. Mr. Y stopped at the doorway near the hallway and turned back to the others.

"Please follow me," commanded the host. Mr. Y raised his hand and snapped his fingers. Instantly, Tony and the others were transported to another location. Mr. Y was positioned to the left of an entrance to a slate blue granite cave with jagged rocks protruding from the ceiling. The cave had two tunnels, one branching hard left and the other slightly turned to the right.

"You will each have sixty seconds to get to the end of the tunnel and adjoining room, turn around and come back, where you'll cross the white line before me," stated Mr. Y. "The rules are as follows. One - if you do not reach the end of the room, you fail the challenge," he stated bluntly. "Two - if you do not cross this white finish line within sixty seconds, you fail the challenge," he continued as he pointed down to the six-inch thick white line just outside the cave's entrance. "And three – if you succeed at the challenge and discuss any aspect of it with another contestant, you'll be disqualified and thereby fail the challenge," he concluded. "Young lady – you are first," stated the magical host as he peered directly into the eyes of the only female contestant.

After a brief smile that raised the right corner of his mouth, Mr. Y snapped his fingers. Instantly, Alison Watson stood ready on top of hard packed snow just under the cave's rocky threshold. She was clothed in a red and white striped full-length ski outfit and bolted onto a pair of cross-country skis with two poles encased within the tight grip of her hands. She pumped her legs in opposite rhythm upward and downward and raised the front of her skis off the snow as she prepped for a race.

"What the hell is happening?" said Tony softly with one eyebrow slightly raised above the other.

"Ready, set, go!" shouted Mr. Y as he clicked the start button on the stopwatch in his left hand. Alison raced into the cave. The ornate time instrument also had a twisted gold rope handle that matched the one around Mr. Y's waist. *Still no feet,* thought Tony as he glanced down under the host.

The group that remained outside the cave's entrance focused their attention on Alison. They leaned in to hear swooshing sounds coming from inside the cave as the young woman disappeared from view. Within ten seconds, the sounds emanating from the cave went quiet and a look of concern and anticipation appeared on each of the group's faces. Thirty-five seconds later, the silence was broken by the distant sound of Alison returning from her round trip. Right before the finish line, she ditched her skis and sprinted across the finish line on foot.

"Oh - too long Ms. Watson," announced Mr. Y as he viewed the stopwatch in his hand. "Sixty-three seconds. You fail," he concluded. The young woman collapsed to the ground in disappointment and subsequently passed out. Tony and the other male contestant stood in silence. Two men in sterile white uniforms with gas masks affixed to their heads appeared from the right entrance of the cave, lifted the collapsed woman up from the snow, and carried her back into the tunnel.

"Where the hell are they taking her?" asked Tony.

"You're next Mr. Blackwell. Good luck," calmly stated Mr. Y as he reset the stopwatch.

Instantly, Tony was standing outside the entrance to the cave and poised to take on a challenge he did not quite understand. He peered into the cave looking first left, then right at both tunnel options. *Should I go left since Alison almost passed the challenge or take the right entrance?* Tony's heart raced with anticipation. With a sign of trepidation, Tony turned back to ask the other contestant a question, but he was gone. The cave's entrance was replaced with an oval hatched door positioned six inches above the ground that stood about five feet tall. Tony stood directly in front of the steel door.

"Can I ask the other guy a question?" said Tony.

"You can ask, but he may not tell you much. Just open the door," replied the host as he pointed to the copper colored metal door. Tony turned the wheel handle on the door until it released the seal and pushed it open. He expected to see the other contestant, but instead saw only clouds with winds blowing heavily away from the door.

The wind was so strong that Tony had a hard time keeping the door open. It was as if he was in an airplane moving forward at well over two hundred miles an hour! Tony moved a bit closer towards the slightly opened door and looked down, only to see the ground a mile below. *How is this possible?*

"What the hell?" muttered Tony as he tightened his grip on the door handle and positioned his left hand against the side of the frame to steady him. He continued to look down at the moving ground below him, astonished at the transition.

"Ready Mr. Blackwell?" asked Mr. Y with somewhat of an impatient look on his face, the stopwatch cleared and poised to start. Tony paused briefly, then closed the hatch and instantly was returned to the starting position in front of the original cave.

"What am I doing here!" screamed Tony at Mr. Y, but didn't get a response. Instead, Mr. Y simply raised the stopwatch to where he could clearly see the timer's face out of his peripheral vision, all while maintaining his view of Tony.

"Ready, set, go!" shouted Mr. Y after an awkward three second stare. *Click.*

Tony sprinted down the left path of the tunnel on skis. His heart raced while his arms pumped with clenched fists on the poles as he increased his speed. He slightly leaned to the left to follow the gradual bend in the cave's pathway. The narrow ceiling and walls were carved out of dirt and jagged stone, making it dangerous to move at high speeds. Regardless, Tony raced as fast as he could. Simple, light fixtures hung from the ceiling at intervals of fifteen feet to provide a dim but necessary light.

Blackwell arrived at the end of the tunnel, which connected the cave to a large auditorium room with a very high ceiling. At the far end of the room was an elevated stage positioned five feet above the floor. It was made of lacquered dark mahogany wood, but showed the typical wear of a schoolroom auditorium. Black curtains were drawn closed, leaving a narrow runway section of the stage exposed. *This must be the end of the room,* thought Tony. He walked into the room at a brisk pace and towards the stage, eyes probing left and right for any risks in the room.

"Just touch the stage and get the hell out of here," he spoke softly. There were more than a hundred people inside the room, most sitting at long tables suitable for a school lunchroom.

"B – 9," announced a well-dressed middle-aged man sitting at a basic table near the front left side of the room. The declaration echoed over the room's speaker system. *They're all playing Bingo.*

"Stay focused and just get to the end," he muttered to himself as Tony continued to the end of the auditorium. As he got closer to the stage, he looked up and saw four people hanging from the ceiling from what appeared to be braided ropes tied around their ankles. The white ropes were linked to a complicated and interconnected pulley system mounted on the ceiling. The pulleys and ropes traversed the entire ceiling.

"What the hell!" shouted Tony as he slowed his pace. *Something is wrong.*

"Now!" shouted the man with the microphone, who moments before was calling the Bingo game. Tony firmly slapped his hand on the stage, turned, and sprinted out of the room as fast as he could.

The floor suddenly became covered with a series of intertwined ropes that slithered like young Albino Spotted pythons. Several monkeys strategically located on three sides of the room began pulling on large ropes connected to the ceiling-based pulley system. Tony pumped his arms and sprinted.

"Pull faster!" called the announcer. The monkeys responded immediately and pulled down harder and faster on the ropes hanging in front of them. As Tony ran, he noticed that the ropes began to rise off the floor.

"You bastards are trying to trap me!" shouted Tony at the announcer with disbelief in his tone. One of the ropes caught Tony's right foot and caused him to trip.

"Not today boys," muttered Tony as he quickly used both hands to free his shoe from his foot and the rising ropes. The Bingo participants all cheered in support of the monkeys. Once Tony broke free of the snare, he sprinted out of the room like a football player running through a tire drill, knees pumping high to avoid being caught by the snake-like ropes.

The volume in the room rose to an almost deafening level as the chaos unfolded. Tony reached the cave again and stopped briefly to look at both tunnel options – left and right. In an instant, he turned right and ran through the tunnel that he had used before. This time the inside was different. The entire tunnel was cut out of ice, with the floor still covered in packed snow.

"What the hell is going on?" shouted Tony as he moved quickly through the tunnel, frequently slipping over the snow. As he rounded the last corner leading towards the start of the tunnel, he noticed that the tunnel had narrowed considerably.

"Go get him!" ordered the man with the microphone. The small army of monkeys sprinted into the tunnel that Tony had chosen. Hearing the announcement, Tony pressed forward, but didn't know if he could outrun the mammals. The tunnel ahead of him continued to narrow with every blink of his eyes. *This can't be happening to me.*

The monkeys raced through the right tunnel and expertly maneuvered over the snow using arm-length pick axes like professional skiers use poles. The full-grown male primates stood approximately three feet tall. They were covered in thick grayish brown hair. Long tails helped the monkeys navigate as they continued to move at alarming speeds through the tunnel chasing Tony.

Each monkey wore matching purple shorts, vests, and fez hats strapped to their chins, adorned with black accents in the shape of a triangle. Several racing monkeys exposed sharp teeth as they screeched in hot pursuit of their human target. The tunnel continued to narrow as

Tony attempted to finish the race. He was forced to drop to his knees and crawl. By the sound of the chaos echoing behind him, Tony knew the monkeys were gaining on him and would catch him shortly.

"Come on Blackwell," grunted Tony as he used every bit of energy to keep moving as fast as he could through the still narrowing tunnel. The sound of the monkeys got increasingly louder. They hooted and hollered as they closed in on him. The sound of clattering steel pierced the packed snow and echoed like a well-timed symphony in Tony's mind. *Pandemonium.*

"Dammit!" shouted Tony as he was forced to move from a crawl to a horizontal position, lying flat on his stomach. He used his arms and hands to reach out as far forward as possible, and then pull his outstretched body, dangling legs and all, through the tunnel a foot at a time. The tunnel shrank to two feet high and appeared to still be narrowing. *How is this possible?*

Tony could no longer see any light at the end of the tunnel. He turned to look back, only to see the ice monkeys approaching quickly. A dozen of them were only twenty feet away. The dangling lights above the widest part of the tunnel behind him flickered as they swung in synchronous motions. As he continued to look at the approaching raging troop of monkeys, his eyes lit up in a panic as splashes of light and darkness played like a silent film.

"Shit!" Tony cried out as he continued to pull his almost lifeless body through the tunnel a foot at a time. *They will be here in seconds*, thought Tony as he struggled to keep moving forward. *Pull, pull!*

2 – THE BEGINNING

The pulsing siren of the alarm clock jolted Tony from his monkey-raged dream. He rolled to the side and reached across the bed with his left hand and slapped his palm down on the alarm clock snooze button, silencing the screeching and repetitive annoyance. It was 6:15 a.m. and Mr. Blackwell had an important presentation to give today. Sleep was becoming more exhausting, but Tony needed to focus on his career at the bank this morning.

"What the hell was that about?" questioned Tony as he contemplated his recent dream. Sweat beaded across his body from forehead to chest. "Time to rock and roll buddy," continued Tony as he wiped the sweat off his face with his forearm. There was no time to dawdle today, strange dream or not.

Tony energetically sprung out of bed and headed towards the bathroom for a shower. A red and white Boston Red Sox shower curtain hung from the shower rod. Tony pushed the plastic aside and slowly adjusted the chrome nozzle, causing water to pulsate from the shower head. Even though he had only been in Boston for six years, Tony had been transformed, as most in Bean Town, to an avid Red Sox fan. As water pulsed into the shower, the heat caused the mirror above the sink to fill with steam. Tony shed his linen pajama pants and swiped his hand over the fogged mirror. He glanced at himself in the mirror and playfully slapped his stomach twice.

"Got to stay fit," he boasted. "You have softball practice after work. Got to look good for Melissa," he continued as he reached for the iPod blaster sitting on the sink counter. Within moments of pressing the play button, Bon Jovi's "Living on a Prayer" filled the room with classic Jersey rock and roll. Tony stepped into the shower and pulled the curtain closed. He buried his head under the hot steamy water and closed his eyes for a few moments as the water raced down his face.

Reflecting on his recent dream, he re-imagined the unpleasant details of the furry troop of angry primates chasing him through the winding ice tunnel. After wiping the clean water from his face and slicking back his jet-black hair, Tony began to sing along with Jon Bon Jovi, echoing the lead singer's poetic words. The day had officially begun as New Jersey rock and roll vibrated through the air and coursed through Tony's veins.

Even though he now lived in Boston, Tony never forgot his roots growing up in New Jersey. He was raised in Flemington, an upper middle-income bedroom community famous for the Lindbergh trial. Flemington was also a bedroom community to global telecommunications and pharmaceutical firms. AT&T, Merck, and Johnson & Johnson headquarters were all no more than twenty minutes away. As a teenager, Tony performed well as an A-minus student athlete, who had a talent for math and computers. His father was a successful pilot for United Airlines, while his mother stayed at home with Tony and his sisters, and served as a substitute teacher at the town's middle school.

Tony had two older sisters, each now with several children of their own. Lisa and Lauri lived a typical middle-income lifestyle after college. Both lived within the New Jersey, Pennsylvania area and stayed close to their childhood roots.

Early in high school and throughout college, Tony leveraged his analytical gift. He could visualize problems and solutions *three-dimensionally*. He quickly separated himself from other students with his achievements in math and technology. By the end of high school, Tony set his sights on the Massachusetts Institute of Technology for college, with aspirations of continuing on to flight school and becoming an aviator like his father.

Tony was accepted into MIT and succeeded academically. The five years, which included a cooperative education internship at a classified think-tank, went by quickly. The program was not easy and included many moments of academic pain and persistence. Tony pulled at least one all-night studying session every *two weeks* for the *last two years*. He established a routine of studying, exercise, and mind-freeing motorcycle rides. The motorcycle was, of course, purchased without his father's knowledge. Guilt crept in, and Tony finally sat down with his father and told him about the bike. His dad, also a motorcycle rider, was all too relieved with the news, as he feared his son had gotten some young woman on campus pregnant. They both laugh about that day from time to time.

Upon graduation, Tony enrolled in the U.S. Navy's Officer Candidate School, commonly called OCS, with the anticipation of continuing to the Navy flight program. His father had been a Navy fighter pilot before joining United Airlines, flying the venerable F-14 Tomcat, equipped with the M61A-1 20mm Vulcan Gatlin gun and a barrage of AIM-9 Sidewinder, AIM7 Sparrow missiles. Photos of Navy fighter jets in formation above U.S. carrier ships adorn the walls of his parents' home in New Jersey. His father's service included time with the VF-2 Bounty Hunters squadron, call sign *Bullets*, on the *USS Enterprise* (CVN-65), the *USS Ranger* (CV-61), and the *USS Kitty Hawk* (CV-63), protecting America's assets around the world.

Shortly into OCS, Tony realized he would not make the Navy's elite flight team because of inferior vision. No doubt, the damn computers and all those late nights running math simulations on MIT's powerful computers had an impact. In the end, the only thing his MIT degree was not going to get him was a coveted pair of Navy gold wings like his old man.

After the Navy informed Tony that he would not be admitted into the flight program, Tony had to make a choice, quit or serve four years as a Navy officer. Joining the Navy without flying wasn't what Tony had planned. He needed to find another path or Drop on Request, *DOR* in Navy lingo, from Officer Candidate School. He had never quit anything in his life, but this was different. He had to figure out what he was going to do with his life.

Tony made his decision after a frank consultation with his father. He successfully completed the OCS program and entered the U.S. Navy as an Ensign Cryptologic Warfare Officer. Tony spent the next four years overseeing enlisted sailors who worked as Cryptologic Technicians. Their role was to collect, analyze, and report on real-time signal intelligence. The more interesting role was to develop and acquire cutting-edge exploitation and defense systems. In short, Tony helped the United States military advance its offense by weakening our enemy's capabilities through the use of math and technology.

The *New York Times* reported a technological success when the Israeli military deployed the Stuxnet virus against Iranian nuclear power control systems. Stuxnet put the Iranian nuclear weapons program behind schedule by at least two years. It was never proved, but Stuxnet was thought to have been conceived and developed by the United States military. *Classified secrets stay secret unless stolen or leaked by traitors.* Tony's job was to protect them.

After serving four years and promoted to the officer rank of O-3 lieutenant, Tony left the U.S. Navy and set his sights on the private sector. After a series of interviews with a variety of firms in Boston and Washington, D.C., Tony settled on a high paying actuary position at the prestigious Bank of America. Even though his MIT degree and mathematical prowess did not get him into the cockpit of a U.S. Navy fighter jet, Tony was confident he was on his way to a well paying and happy career. Math was at the core of who he was and how he analyzed life. *How can I not be happy playing with math every day and being paid as an actuary?*

Tony walked to the closet, his hair still wet from the shower, and selected a crisp suit for the day. Just then, the phone rang, barely audible over the classic rock and roll music.

"Good morning Melissa," Tony answered after peering at the caller-id and simultaneously lowering the stereo's volume via the remote control pointed towards the bathroom. "I missed you last night," he continued.

"I missed you too, but you told me not to come over so you could prepare for your big presentation," returned Melissa as she intentionally exaggerated Tony's annoying habit of putting work first.

"You know how important this presentation is to me today, right?"

"Yeah, I'm just kidding," she returned with a slight giggle. "I know it means a lot to you sweetie and I really do hope you get that promotion," she continued as she backed off her initial prodding. "Hey, do you want to grab a cup of coffee before work and meet me at the T?" she asked cautiously.

"Sure. Let me shave and I'll meet you at the Park Street Station stop in twenty-five minutes," replied Tony in his typical warm manner.

"Ok. You know that I love you," returned Melissa, changing the topic a bit towards their relationship.

"Yes and I love you too sugar," replied Tony as he started to crank up the music again. "If I'm going to be on time, I have to go," he stated. "See you in a bit," continued Tony as the music volume mounted and he mouthed a kiss into the phone's handset before putting it back into the cradle.

Melissa smiled and hung up the phone, knowing that she had met the man she was going to marry. *Tony was special*, she thought. *Not like most of the other MIT nerds. Kind, smart, and gentle.*

Tony raced to the bathroom for a quick shave. Afterwards he put on his blue pinstripe business suit, selected just the right pink power tie, and grinned with confidence as he adjusted the tie knot in the mirror.

Tony grabbed his classic black leather briefcase and headed for the street.

Melissa as usual, was on time and waiting for Tony as he approached the entrance to the above ground subway station that would take them both to the heart of Boston's financial center and beyond.

"Hey, you!" stated Melissa, holding two cups of coffee. Putting them down on the park bench, she reached for Tony and gave him a kiss. "You look fabulous," she continued as she lovingly reached up to adjust his tie. Not that anything was wrong with it, but she wanted Tony to know just how much she cared for him and often used a variety of techniques to get close to him. "Perfect," she concluded after tightening the knot just a bit. Afterwards, she placed a hand flat on Tony's chest and patted down the silk masterpiece.

"Thanks M. You have a heart of gold," he stated warmly as he returned a kiss, pausing slightly before actually touching her lips. Tony could sense her melting right in front of him. He liked being in control. Melissa surprised him and moved in for the kill, kissing him first.

When the trolley arrived at Park Street, they both eagerly jumped aboard and marked a spot where they could stand together on the crowded subway car. Within minutes, the T's trolley submersed from its above ground venue and retreated into the dark and ominous tunnels below the city of Boston.

With one hand on the overhead strap and the other holding her coffee, Melissa smiled as she looked at Tony. "Do well today," she stated.

Tony reached out for his girlfriend and gave her a quick kiss. "Thanks M. I love you," he gushed with a sinister smile. As the trolley slowed at his stop, he smiled at Melissa before de-boarding the trolley car. His T stop was three before Melissa's stop and he needed to get to the office to prepare.

3 – THE GRIND

Tony sat quietly at his desk and reviewed the PowerPoint he was going to present to his vice president later in the morning. He cautiously and meticulously inspected each slide and made small corrections in grammar and content to get the document just perfect.

"Hey dude! Are you ready for the big meeting?" asked one of his best friends and work colleagues as he entered Tony's cubicle.

"Hey Richie," Tony replied, as he looked up to see his co-worker. "Almost there," he continued as he rapidly typed on the computer keyboard and saved the minor revision to his data key.

"Come on man. You need to take a break and get more relaxed before you go *into* the show," mocked Richie as he pulled Tony's chair away from the computer. "I'm buying if you want a decent cup of Java," he continued. "You know I can't stand the black joe in this place."

Tony broke from his concentration and looked up at his friend. "Ok. I could use a break. Thanks Richie," he concluded and rose from his chair to give Richie a crisp high-five. "Let's go. I have thirty minutes to spare."

The pair navigated the cubicles on the floor, then rode the elevator to the first floor lobby of the high-rise commercial building. Richie scanned the lobby for women as they walked. Tony did not even notice the several attractive, professional women looking towards the well-dressed pair as they walked. Richie noticed and talked incessantly, as he always did. The close friends walked out of the building and onto the bustling sidewalk on Federal Street. A Starbucks was conveniently located nearby.

As the pair waited in line, Richie continued to scan the landscape for attractive women.

"Two black coffees please," asked Richie upon reaching the counter. Starbucks was always bustling at this time of the day. "You haven't listened to a *damn* thing I said on our walk over here," stated Richie. "Did you see those hot chicks in the lobby checking us out? Which one should I go after?" he continued.

"Who? Which ones?"

"Are you *kidding* me? Do *not* tell me you didn't even notice them! What about the redhead and those two hot brunettes with short cocktail skirts?" continued Richie. "Oh God, I love the way women dress in this city. Short skirts and roaming eyes that make it look like they are always on the prowl." After a brief pause when he realized Tony was not on the same topic, he continued. "Never mind man. You have Melissa," muttered Richie with a bit of sarcasm. "What does she really see in you anyway?" he continued with a complimentary grin on his face. Tony shook his head slowly and broke into a small smile.

"I've been spending too much time in the office and working late at night for this presentation," returned Tony.

"I am pretty sure it will go just fine Tony," said Richie as he patted his friend's shoulder. "Now, on to more important things." Tony turn around to face his friend. "Are we on for happy hour tonight at the Hong Kong?" asked Richie, repeatedly jabbing a finger into Tony's chest.

"Sure. 9:00 p.m." Tony looked his friend squarely in the eyes. "Melissa will be there by 10:00 p.m. if that is ok?" he continued, squinting slightly as he looked for his friend's approval.

"You're so *whipped*," replied Richie as he rolled his eyes, jealousy at the core of his comment.

"Thanks buddy. I really like her. You know that right?"

"I know. We *all* know. Jesus Christ! Enough already about Melissa. Let's case the chicks in this place so I can clear my head before going back upstairs to my mundane job," ranted Richie.

"You *are* girl crazy Richie," said Tony.

"You're *damn* right I am," returned Richie with his trademark charismatic smile. His smile and all around attractiveness could melt the clothes off of the majority of Boston's single women, and some of the married ones.

Richie Carini grew up in Atlantic City, New Jersey. A star lacrosse player with a mediocre grade point average got him admitted to Syracuse University in New York on an athletic scholarship. Richie was six feet tall with an athletic build, piercing green eyes, and wavy brown hair. Many on the Syracuse lacrosse team often joked about his South-Philly haircut. Richie took it in strike and always prevailed, though. His wavy hair pushed back over the ear, slicked back from his forehead, and flowed backwards until it curved off the top of his shirt collar. That look, combined with his athletic grace and confidence, usually resulted in him secretly stealing teammate girlfriends away for a night or two.

The friends spent the next fifteen minutes drinking their morning brew, talking about the company softball team, and discussing the Boston Red Sox's upcoming schedule. Richie and Tony engaged in a playful discussion, all while Richie continued to scan the Starbucks seating area for his next opportunity of love at first sight. *Life was good,* thought Tony.

* * *

Forty-five minutes later and fully caffeinated, Tony stood in front of the conservative audience of bank executives and peers. "Thank you for coming this morning ladies and gentlemen," he said as he handed out printed color slides of his full presentation. Over the next thirty minutes, Tony captivated the room as he walked through his introduction and presentation body, highlighting fifty years of actuary premiums, payouts, and revenue for the bank. Richie watched from outside the conference room, peering through the vertical window that ran the length of the door.

"While this has been a stable revenue stream for our bank, I believe that we can still increase our revenue dramatically," Tony continued as he advanced the presentation to the next page. He revealed the details of his new mathematical model and recommended approach.

Carl Roberts, Vice President of the actuarial department, had been flipping through Tony's presentation deck during the meeting. Mr. Roberts sat upright in his chair. Several of his subordinates who flanked him on either side took notice of the posture change. The expression on his face was clear, stern disappointment.

"My analysis of our portfolio indicates that there is an opportunity for the bank to increase income by raising the rates after normal life expectancy across various age and health categories," Tony continued. "Americans are living longer today. This is a fact. My proposed change means that we will be able to significantly increase our profits for those who beat life expectancy ages," said Tony confidently as he presented an overlapping bar chart representing the data behind his model.

"Do you really think our customers will pay more for this premium Mr. Blackwell?" interjected Roberts. "This recent recession really took a bite out of our income when a portion of our clients canceled their policies. Today, only the fairly wealthy clients can still afford to plan for the death of a loved one or themselves."

Tony took a breath. "Well, Mr. Roberts," stated Tony.

"Stop right there Mr. Blackwell. I am responsible for the revenue stream and profits associated with this portfolio at the Bank of America and I think I have heard enough today," he interrupted as he placed the colorful handout on the table. "I read through your numbers as you were presenting and I have some issues with your assumptions and conclusions. Before we think of charging our clients, who are pretty damn savvy, a single penny more, I think we need some additional analysis and clarification on some of your assumptions," he stated boldly staring directly at Tony. "Tony, this all looks good on paper, but it is not as much an analysis as it is a *speculation*," he continued in a softer and more mentoring tone, condescending albeit. "Go back and find somebody in the industry that has done this before and been successful at raising revenue and I will take another look," he concluded as he stood up.

"Mr. Roberts. Nobody else has done this type of analysis and increase before," interjected Tony. "We would be the first to market. What a great opportunity to lead."

"Which is precisely the position I cannot put this prestigious institution in my young colleague," responded Roberts.

"I understand," replied Tony with a dejected look on his face. Robert's subordinates also rose after their superior and followed him out of the meeting room, prematurely ending the presentation and setting an awkward vibe for those still sitting in the room.

"Nice work," muttered one of Robert's minions as he paused during his walk past Tony. "Concrete facts and proven analytics," he whispered. "That is what Mr. Roberts wants. Not speculation," he continued, clearly showing his allegiance to Carl Roberts. "Roberts doesn't want trailblazers here, just consistent earnings without excessive risks," he concluded, patting Tony on the shoulder twice. "Consistent earnings," he repeated, this time in a much softer tone.

"Old-school Harvard bankers," muttered Tony after all the participants had left the room. Tony just stood there silently with his presentation still on the screen and nobody there to see it. "Shit!" he grunted loudly as he turned to shut down the computer. Tony walked in silence back to his cube. With lips pursed and showing signs of stress, he sat down in his office chair and stared at the blank computer screen.

4 – HONG KONG

At 9:45 p.m., the renowned Hong Kong bar in Cambridge had been already in full swing.

"Shit Tommy, order another *Bowl*," yelled Richie from halfway across the room as he walked towards the rest room. Tommy acknowledged with a simple thumbs-up and turned to signal the bartender. He was part of a contingency from the bank that often frequented the bar, commonly packed with a young college crowd, mainly from Harvard and MIT. The pub was a great way for students to decompress from the stress of an Ivy League education. The run down pub sat just above an even more run down Chinese restaurant known for some of the best

Cantonese and Szechuan take-out in town. Every once in a while, patrons would see a Hollywood star dining in one of the dimly lit corners of the establishment. Hollywood filmed a variety of movies and TV shows in and around the Cambridge area, especially near the Charles River separating Cambridge from downtown Boston.

The evening ramped up quickly as scores of young twenty and thirty-some things filled the bar, to dine on the establishment's famous drink – the dreaded *Scorpion Bowl*. The house favorite was comprised of nine different shots of liquor that flowed down the throat as easily as a non-alcoholic Hawaiian Punch drink. The Scorpion Bowl was a silent and dangerous concoction. First-time guests were always the most fun to watch. They would typically drink a *Bowl* and not know they were completely drunk until they stood up. The locals always got a kick watching vacationers experiment with the famous quaff.

Tony looked at his watch. Melissa would be arriving shortly. He could not wait to see her, especially given his shitty day at work. Tony never complained, but did rely on the compassion of a few close people in his life. Melissa was one such person. In the meantime, he and his high-priced financial friends floundered about the day's work as if they were all in dead end jobs. *We're so lucky,* thought Tony.

"Hey Tony. I think Carl Roberts is an idiot!" shouted Charlie Coleman from across the table. "He's so afraid of taking a risk, he probably still sleeps with the lights on and has sex with his wife in just the missionary position," he harassed. Charlie followed his criticism by taking a long drag from his Scorpion Bowl through the long straw protruding from the local cocktail. "Wow," he huffed after downing the local potion, shaking his head back and forth. "Whew!"

"I cannot believe that Roberts just stopped the presentation," mused Tony as he returned the comment over the top of the music playing in the background. "I have to redo the numbers and hit him again," he continued.

"Not giving up Blackwell are you?" asked Lucy, another bank co-worker. "I like that about you," she continued as she flashed Tony a wicked smile that curled only part way up her rosy Asian cheeks. Lucy worked in the accounting office and often would go out of her way to talk to Tony in the actuary office section.

"Are you flirting with me Lucy?" smiled Tony.

"You bet I am, but I know the good ones are already taken. Melissa is the lucky one," mused Lucy.

"Do you really think I am going to give up on this idea?" asked Tony in defense. "I know that I am right and Roberts is going to learn it one way or another," he continued, raising the entire coconut shelled Bowl to the cheers of his friends. Tony took a long swig from the straw. "If I cannot convince Roberts, I will go above him or will drive it somewhere else," stated Tony as he built up more confidence with every swallow of the potent cocktail.

"You are crazy," interjected Richie as he sat down at the table. "That could get you fired man!" he stated, followed by a dual-straw drag from a Scorpion Bowl directly in front of him.

"I will either do it in this bank or find another. I know Roberts is conservative and smart, but I am way smarter than that dinosaur," continued Tony. Melissa walked through the front door and immediately caught the attention of Tony.

"M!" he called towards the door, standing to get her attention. Melissa scanned the room until she found him. Her facial expression melted as soon as she saw Tony from across the room and began to move towards him. Tony left the table and walked across the room to meet her in the midst of the pub's growing and rowdy crowd.

"Hey, how are you?" asked Melissa as she softly clasped his hands in hers and placed a soft kiss on Tony's lips.

"I have been better," replied Tony as he pulled away and hung his head. "I got slaughtered in the presentation today," he continued as he raised their clasped hands towards his chest. "Carl Roberts interrupted the presentation and got up and left. I am smarter than he gives me credit for," concluded Tony.

"I know that sweetie, but you have got to know how to play these office politics. For Christ sake, Carl Roberts is your boss's boss." Melissa then placed a gentle kiss on Tony's cheek. "Don't mess with him."

"Yeah, yeah. I get it," replied Tony as he directed her towards the table where their friends were waiting. "Come on. I want to forget about this for a while. My friends at the bank have been talking about it for way too long tonight."

"Melissa! What took you so long?" called Richie as he glanced at his watch, which read precisely 10:00 p.m. "Right on time," he smiled as he reached out to give his best friend's girlfriend a kiss on the cheek. "Lucy, how about ordering another drink for our friend M?" continued Richie as he arranged a chair for Melissa to join the group.

Over the next hour, the group of highly educated yuppies discussed everything from challenges at work, local politics, company softball, and the best pitchers on the Red Sox as they drank the night away. Scorpion Bowls continued to flow as the friends and the discussion became one.

She's mesmerizing to watch, thought Tony as he listened to Melissa talk about Tony and a day in the life of an education professional.

Melissa Stewart was a Boston native who grew up in Somerville, attended

Northeastern University and obtained a bachelor's degree in elementary education. Now at the Park Street Elementary School in the Northeast side of the city, she worked as a fourth grade teacher in a very well respected private school. She didn't fit the profile of everyone else at the pub table and was not particularly fond of the aggressive Boston financial sector type-A personalities that the area commonly attracted. Tony was different, however.

As Melissa partook in the evening's conversation, she saw that Tony could not keep his eyes off of her. At five feet six inches and one hundred and twenty pounds fit, her auburn hair fell to grace the tops of her shoulders. Melissa reached into her purse and put on her glasses to see the menu more clearly. She often sported her pair of stylish tortoise shell glasses. In addition to improving her vision, the corrective lenses gave her a very sexy librarian look, softening her shell even more.

As the night progressed, Tony grew tired with the venue and the abundant amount of alcohol consumed. He reached below the table and touched Melissa's hand on her lap and gave her a subtle wink. *It is time to go* he silently communicated.

"Listen guys, I have to be at school early tomorrow morning for meetings," stated Melissa as she rose to say goodbye to Tony's friends.

"Yeah, yeah honey. We get it," replied Richie as he raised his glass of beer that only minutes ago replaced the Scorpion Bowl he had devoured. "Tony, take her home will you?" he continued now standing as he moved towards his friend for a hug.

"You're drunk," laughed Tony as he rose to meet his friend. They embraced with a solid hug, each patting the other on the back repeatedly. Melissa laughed as she looked on and grabbed Tony's hand to lead him out of the famous pub.

"That I am Mr. Blackwell," shot back Richie as he took a bow, finessed with his left arm raised high and his right arm draped across his waist. "Don't worry about Roberts," whispered Richie. "I can have one of my family members take care of that idiot," he laughed, referring to his Italian heritage and assumed link to the Mafia. "I have a feeling that he is going to have an accident going to work one day," Richie slurred, slightly wobbling from side to side. Tony just smiled, knowing that Richie had too much to drink and that the alcohol was now taking its course.

"Go home Richie and get some rest," returned Tony. "Come on M. Let's blow this place," he continued and escorted her out of the local watering hole. As the pair made their way through the thick crowd, Melissa briefly turned back to the table of friends and waved before Tony whisked her out the front door, down the stairs, through part of the Chinese restaurant, and finally to the street.

It was late and neither Tony, nor Melissa wanted to wait for the T to get home. Tony flagged down a taxi and opened the door for his girlfriend. "Fifty-nine Phillips Street please," exhaled Tony as he climbed in after Melissa and pulled the door shut. The ride back to Tony's apartment was relatively quick. Melissa cuddled up next to him and put her head down on his left shoulder.

"Thanks for asking me to come tonight Tony," she spoke. The two had been dating for almost two years and looked fully integrated as a couple.

"You helped move the conversation from me to you Melissa. Thank *you*," he whispered, turning slightly to his left to face her.

"You are welcome Mr. Blackwell," Melissa returned. "Just make me one promise Tony," she continued. "That you will never give up," she said. "Everybody gets knocked down every once in a while – even you," continued Melissa. "Just don't be like the rest of society and quit," she concluded.

"*Never give up,*" he whispered softly as he stared through the taxi's windshield. Liking his response, Melissa wrapped her arm around Tony's midsection and squeezed him tight. Within ten minutes, the pair arrived back in Brookline and exited the cab. Tony tipped the cabby an extra five dollars for his efforts. He always respected other professions, especially blue-collar jobs and made it a point to tip for good service. He never wanted to be viewed as *better* than others and never took for granted his rise from the academic elite of MIT.

The pair trudged to Tony's apartment, hand in hand. "I'm beat," explained Tony as he opened the door to his comfortable little apartment, which was sparsely decorated but clean. Tony lived alone in a quaint one-bedroom unit where the living room doubled as an office, laptop computer prominently affixed on top of the desk. His computer technology was also integrated directly into a forty-two inch plasma screen on the wall near his black leather couch. "I am going to grab a quick shower if you don't mind and head to bed," he stated to Melissa as he headed towards the bathroom. "Feel free to grab what floats your boat in the fridge," he continued, winking towards her as she sat down on the couch.

"Ok," replied Melissa confidently, but quietly. She had other plans.

5 - LANCELOT

Once Tony was comfortably inside the bathroom, Melissa headed to the bedroom. She opened the drawer of the table next to the bed and reached for a pack of matches. The black matchbox was labeled with the prestigious Ruth Chris brand steak house. Tony and his Bank of America friends often frequented the swanky steak joint conveniently located in the financial district. The bank often scheduled the venue for lunch and dinner with clients. It was just another reminder of how far and fast Tony had risen in the short years since graduating from MIT and serving as an officer in the U.S. Navy.

Melissa also found two tea candles inside the drawer, conveniently wrapped with glass containers. She had given them as a gift. She struck a single match and lit both candles, providing a romantic ambiance to the otherwise stark male room.

Melissa pulled back the white duvet cover and sheet on the queen bed and folded it at an angle as if to invite Tony to bed. She promptly got undressed, sprinkled some of her garments on the floor, starting with her black brassiere at the bathroom entrance, followed by socks, then her blouse leading to the bedroom. Stripped down to her matching black panties, Melissa climbed into the bed and pulled the white cotton sheet up to her chin. Lowering her arms to her waist, she intentionally exposed one of her legs to the side of the duvet cover. Then she waited.

"Did you find anything to eat Melissa?" called Tony from inside the bathroom. Silence was his response. Firmly placing a white towel around his waist, he opened the door and immediately caught the attention of her brassiere on the floor. A small smile came to his tired face. "Is this some kind of trail to the Holy Grail?" he mused.

"Sir Lancelot, save me!" she playfully cried out from the bedroom, followed by a bursting laugh as she pulled the sheet fully over her head.

"I *definitely* should have spent more time studying the history of the Knights of the Round Table in college," laughed Tony as he walked into the living room to turn out the lights. "Guinevere, where are you?" he continued as he moved towards the bedroom. Candles flickered just enough to light the way. "Lancelot reporting for duty," he joked as he entered the bedroom and pulled back the bed sheet, exposing his topless girlfriend in waiting. Melissa seductively and slowly crossed her arms over her breasts, giving Tony just enough time to see what she wanted him to see and then grinned as she stretched out fully lengthwise on the bed, slightly tilting her chin down.

"Duty it is," whispered Melissa with a smile on her face. Her reddish-brown hair playfully rested across her cheeks, as a few loose curls dangled over her shoulders. Tony dove across her prone body, twisting in the air to land beside her, causing her to yelp in surprise.

"Nice candles," he stated confidently with new energy in his expression. "Shall I blow them out?"

"No. Please leave them on," responded Melissa as she reached for him and pulled Tony closer to her. "I like the light from them. It's romantic."

"As you wish," replied Tony as he began kissing her neck and working his way down her well-endowed torso. "As you wish," he repeated as he caressed her body with his hands. Melissa quietly reached over to the side of the bed and pulled the sheet over both of them, leaving only a subdued view of the flickering candles through the silhouetted sheet.

Tony and Melissa made passionate love with the help of two aphrodisiacs, courtesy of the Hong Kong bar and the romantic view provided by the tea candles. Thirty minutes later, the lovers fell asleep. Melissa nestled comfortably into Tony's side with his arm comfortably around her. The only movement in the room was provided by the quiet pair of shadows dancing on the far wall. The candle flames danced the night away, seemingly to flirt with one another in their nocturnal ritual.

Dream Challenge

* * *

The non-descript gentleman finished his observations and documented everything he needed for his current assignment. He had the target name, address, company name, car license plate, and of course – his frequent pubs. Anatoly Sizy had been following Rich Spelling for a week, along with a few other candidate targets. He had made up his mind. This guy was the one. The bar was packed with twenty and thirty-some things who were well on their way to being drunk by 11:00 p.m., even for a work night.

His target was an insipid gentleman, employed as a computer programmer for a major software company. Several male friends, mostly drinking bottled beer, sat at the bar. The mark was drinking his preferred liquor drink with ice. Anatoly approached the bar and sat down to the left of his target. His hands rested on the bar while his eyes searched for the bartender, all while keeping an eye to his right via his peripheral vision on the group of professionals.

"Vodka tonic please," asked Anatoly towards the bartender in perfect English. The Intelligence Service field agent ordered the exact drink as Rich Spelling.

The Russian Foreign Intelligence Service (SVR), the successor to the infamous and *dangerous* KGB, was responsible for conducting human and electronic intelligence outside of Russia, implementing military, economic, and biological espionage, and protecting Russian institutions and their families abroad. Created in December 1991, the SVR was headquartered in the Yasenevo district of Moscow and reports directly to the President of Russia. *Directorate S*, the most dangerous unit, included multiple departments and was responsible for deploying agents in foreign lands, conducting various forms of espionage, and recruiting Russians living in other countries to spy for the Federation.

When the drink came, Anatoly took a sip, and then began flipping through email on his mobile phone. *I should have ordered Stolichnaya Gold*, he thought to himself. Nothing but the Russian vodka was worth the money. Mother Russia would be appalled at his drink selection tonight, but he needed to blend into the environment and look and act like an American.

When Sizy had gotten the fluid level of his drink to the same as the man to his right, he put down his glass on the bar and retrieved a pen from his shirt pocket. After fumbling to write on the napkin in front of him, he put the pen back in his shirt pocket and pulled out another. Anatoly rested his right arm on the bar rail, new pen hovered over his own drink. He slowly pressed the top of the pen with his right thumb.

Instead of pushing out an ink tip, a small clear Jell-O-like cube dropped quietly into the glass. It measured no bigger than a millimeter wide. Afterwards, he swapped the fake pen with a real pen and began to write a list of trivial grocery items on the napkin. As he wrote the list, he waited.

A minute later, Anatoly was rewarded for his patience. His target mark excused himself from the group of friends, got up from the bar, and passed directly behind him on the way to the rest room. The others in his group continued to chat. The Russian placed his left hand on his drink and retrieved his keys from his pocket with his other hand. When the moment was right, he dropped the keys, which ricocheted off the bar stool to his right and landed on the floor in the middle of the group.

"I'm so sorry," said Anatoly as he slightly moved towards the men. They all looked down at the keys on the floor. One even graciously reached down to retrieve the keys. With his left hand, Anatoly swapped drinks with his mark.

"No worries. I've got them," replied one of the men as he walked towards Anatoly and placed them on the bar.

"Thanks," stated the Russian as he took a large swig from his new drink. "I think I have had enough tonight boys," stated Anatoly. The group of friends all laughed. *The package had been successfully delivered.* Anatoly placed his near empty drink on the glossy wooden bar, tossed twenty dollars next to the glass, and walked towards the door. As he moved closer to the door, he could hear the group chanting to buy another round.

"Come on Spelling. Move your ass and get us another round. You are such a *light weight*," called out one of the men. Anatoly allowed himself a brief smile as he reached for the door and left the quaint American pub.

The Russian started his rental car, pulled out of the parking lot, and headed for Rich Spelling's house three miles away. There,

Dream Challenge

Sizy would start the communications uplink device that would pair with the small Russian-made translucent transmitter left in the mark's drink. *Everything will be in place by midnight,* thought the Russian agent.

6 – THE EGYPTIAN CRYPT

Tony and two other challengers stood in an underground room that resembled an ancient Egyptian crypt. The walls were cut from large square stones and perfectly fitted together to form a symmetrical rectangular room. The three challengers stood near motionless on a raised platform that overlooked a slightly submerged and beveled floor. The vault was longer than it was wide, approximately forty feet in length. On the opposite side of the room, a large sarcophagus lay flat on the ground, perpendicular to the side walls. A gold chalice rested on top of the ancient coffin.

The grail glistened from the light provided by a series of torches mounted on the walls.

"What the hell is this creepy place?" barked Tony as he turned to the young woman standing next to him. He recognized her from his last dream.

"I don't know, but I don't like it," replied the young woman as she canvassed the room with her eyes, slowly turning her head as she took in the elements of the dank room. The room was fetid and smelled like a decaying cave.

"You were in my dream last night. What are we doing here again?" Tony looked more closely at her now. *She is beautiful,* Tony thought as he continued his stare. For a moment, he imagined he was somewhere else with her as he continued a longer than normal infatuation gaze.

"I have no idea, but this is my fifth time in one of these stupid dream challenges," she replied, now staring directly at the pit floor below them both. "I'm getting pretty tired of that guy Mr. Y too."

"Five times?" replied Tony. "Holy shit," he said softly as his eyebrows rose in amazement. "What is your name?" asked

Tony as he put his hand on her shoulder in an attempt to comfort her.

"Alison," she replied coldly, showing no emotion towards Tony or his attempt to console her. "Alison Watson," she concluded after a brief and awkward pause.

"I am Tony," he returned as he slowly pulled back his hand. She was an attractive, athletic-looking, beautiful woman who stood at about five feet six inches tall. Alison had a short, smartly styled haircut that shaped her straight blond hair neatly around her face, accenting her piercing blue eyes. She was wearing a pair of crisp designer jeans that fit her shape perfectly, augmented with an Adidas light yellow golf pique shirt. The buttons on her shirt were open, which exposed the ample cleavage accenting her slender frame. As Tony turned to look back towards the ornate casket, he noticed Mr. Y floating to his right.

"Welcome my guests!" opened Mr. Y with his arms extended high in the air, white robe falling slightly over each arm. "For tonight's challenge, you will each have sixty seconds to retrieve the grail from the other side of the room. To finish, you must cross the white line, below your feet," he continued while pointing to the end of the square platform where a faint line was etched into the stone just before it dropped off two feet to the pool-like floor below.

"You may each select from one of the weapons on the wall to help you with your challenge," he stated calmly as he pointed to the rightmost wall. "These items cannot be reused and the selection process will start with you Ms. Watson," continued Mr. Y.

The group turned to see three items hanging on the wall, none of which were there just moments before. The weapons included a torch, a shotgun, and a whip.

Alison looked perplexed at the choices before her and after a brief pause stated, "I will take the torch." Mr. Y motioned with his arm extended towards the weapons rack and the lit torch magically moved through the air until the female contestant reached out to grab the handle.

"Mr. Spelling, what is your venom?" asked Mr. Y firmly. Spelling stood confounded as he weighed the two remaining weapon choices.

"How do you know my name?" asked Rich Spelling. He stood out from the other contestants, but seemed quite comfortable in his techno-surfing attire right down to the black and white checkered Sketchers sneakers. Spelling wore black glasses and had his hair slicked to the side, which gave him the look of a chess-playing academic debater.

"I know all of your names. Now, let's get back to the game tonight shall we?" replied the host.

"I will take the whip, but I have no idea why I selected it," replied the young man, almost counterintuitive to his analytical appearance. Again, Mr. Y gestured towards the wall with an outstretched hand and moved the tan leather weapon through the air until it reached Rich Spelling's hand. Rich unraveled the whip and with the flip of his wrist, sampled the weapon, causing it to extend before snapping back as intended.

"Very nice Mr. Spelling," observed the host as a slight smile broke on his compelling face.

"And you Tony," stated Mr. Y, referring to the first name used in the semi-private conversation between Tony and Alison. "You get the shotgun." Mr. Y raised his arm again and motioned to move the black Winchester twelve-gauge pump action weapon through the air until it reached the third contestant's palms. Tony, who was familiar with firearms, opened the gun's magazine and exposed three shells.

I get only three shots? Tony closed the magazine and pumped the fore stock. The first shell loaded into the gun's chamber – ready to shoot.

"One final bit of information before you all get started," continued Mr. Y. "Your own worst fears will be the force that works against you tonight," concluded the host.

"Shit," muttered Tony as he hung his head down. "I have the wrong weapon," he whispered as he shook his head slightly from side to side in disappointment, lips pressed closely together.

"What does that mean?" asked Alison.

"Ms. Watson. You are up first and might I remind you – this is your fifth challenge attempt. Three more failed attempts and your life will be changed forever," warned the host.

Mr. Y snapped his fingers and readied his stopwatch. Alison cautiously moved to the front of the group and positioned herself just behind the starting line with her torch held outright. As Mr. Y raised the stopwatch up high, Alison closed her eyes and mumbled softly "I am not afraid. I am not afraid," desperately trying not to think about her greatest fear – drowning.

"Ready, set, go!" shouted Mr. Y as he started the stopwatch. Alison opened her eyes to the sound of water rushing into the sunken floor from six large water jets that protruded from the walls. The jets rapidly pumped water into the pool-like floor at a tremendous rate. Alison jumped from the small platform into the water, which quickly approached the height of her knees. Grunting, she continued forward and waded through the rising water as fast as she could, all while holding the lit torch well above her head. By the time she had reached three quarters of the way across the room, the water had risen to her chest and continued to rise. The swirling and rising water caused Alison to slow her progress and stumble a bit, her face briefly meeting the rising deluge.

As Alison reached the other side of the room, she quickly placed the torch on the raised ledge before climbing out of the water and grabbing the gold grail. By the time she turned around to reenter the water, it was well above five feet in height and still rising rapidly throughout the entire pit. Grasping the torch in one hand and the grail in the other, Alison jumped back into the water for the return trip back to the podium, holding each object high above her head. Within moments, she was submersed in water, head tilted back, and gasping for air. The torch fell out of her hand and flamed out as she attempted to swim. Alison gulped large amounts of water as she fought for her life.

"I can't breathe. Somebody help me!" she gasped between dunks in the water, not making any additional forward progress towards the finish line. Tony jumped off the ledge into the water and swam towards Alison. By the time he reached her, Alison's head was fully under water. He dove underneath the surface, found her arm and pulled her to the surface in a technique often used by lifeguards.

"Ah," gasped Alison as she sucked in a gulp of air. "Oh my God," she continued as she threw her arms around Tony as he rescued her out of the tumultuous water pit.

"Sixty seconds," interrupted Mr. Y. He clicked the stopwatch, and with his voice raised to pierce the loud noise of the rushing water stated, "You failed Ms. Watson."

Instantly, the water jets stopped pumping water into the pit. A loud noise combined with increased air pressure in the room caused the water in the pit to recede at a pace faster than with which it was filled. Several large circular water cyclones appeared at the base of the floor as the water quickly drained out of the room. Within moments, the water was gone and the normal air pressure restored to the room. Alison lay on the damp floor in tears, still grasping the grail. With the snap of Mr. Y's fingers, the young female contestant fell comatose and slowly released her grip on the chalice until it rolled out of the palm of her hand to the wet ground. With the stroke of Mr. Y's hand, Alison rose from the floor and disappeared from sight through a door that opened at the intersection of two wall joints. Tony Blackwell and Rich Spelling simply stared in amazement.

"Mr. Spelling – you are up," stated Mr. Y as he reset his stopwatch. Rich Spelling cautiously moved to the front of the platform in front of Tony and mentally prepared for his challenge. Rich tucked the rolled whip firmly into his belt to secure it and repeatedly clapped his hands together, indicating that he was ready for the challenge.

"Ready, set, go!" commanded the host. Instantly, eight six-inch wide steel pipes slid out from the side walls, four per side, and spit fire towards the center of the room from a variety of heights and timing. Spelling stood motionless for a brief moment as he attempted to time the sequences of the bursting flames.

One, two, three, counted Rich to himself repeatedly as the front-most flames erupted exactly on the count of two. Spelling jumped down from the platform and stepped past the first row of flames in between bursts. He had successfully passed the first of four flame thrower obstacles. The second set of flames fired at the height of his knees, faster than the first set. After trying to time his next move, Rich determined the bursts were coming too fast, so he dove over the flames in mid-burst and executed a perfect shoulder roll to finish in a standing position. Tony smiled.

"I think he may actually make it," said Tony as Mr. Y turned to acknowledge his statement with a brief, but sinister smile.

The next two sets of flames were firing at a faster pace at more challenging heights. Rich Spelling counted aloud to time the bursts, but clearly did not feel comfortable enough to move.

"One, two, three," counted Spelling as he timed the bursts of fire once again. On the second third count, he ducked and darted forward several yards before stopping before the next fire hazard. The fourth fire hazard spat bright yellow and white flames at different heights from each side of the room. Spelling paused, and then stepped over the lower burst of flames while ducking his head to avoid the upper flames.

Clearing the last hazard, Rich ran fifteen feet to reach the large sarcophagus. He reached down and unsecured the whip from his belt all while keeping his eye on the grail in front of him. After a practice crack of the whip to the side, parallel to the caustic fire, Rich turned towards the grail. He took a deep breath and snapped the whip towards the center of the sarcophagus elevated above him on a platform that did not exist when he started his challenge. The leather wrapped firmly around the grail as intended. Rich jerked hard on the whip and with a single motion, caused the grail to hurl towards him in the air. Spelling reached up to grasp his prize, but the grail came too fast and hit his free arm before falling to the ground. He quickly picked up the chalice and turned around to map his route back.

"Go Spelling!" shouted Tony. "Time is running out!" he continued raising his voice so that Spelling could hear him over the loud and synchronous spits of fire.

Rich reversed course with the same methods he had employed to get to the far end of the room, first stepping over while ducking past the first set of spitting flames. Once past his first obstacle, Spelling repeated his technique through the other three dangers and reached the starting platform. Out of breath, he raced towards the finish line. Spelling quickly climbed the short wall and crossed the white line with the grail secured in one hand.

"Fifty-eight seconds Mr. Spelling," announced Mr. Y. "Well done indeed," he concluded.

Tony reached out to high five his new colleague and competitor. Rich Spelling had a huge smile on his face. Within moments of Spelling's success, an elegant middle-aged woman appeared wearing an ancient Roman white *stola* and red *palla* from a stone door that opened from the side of the room. The woman had long brown hair and wore a pair of matching gold arm bands. She moved elegantly, but quickly towards Rich Spelling. As the Roman beauty moved across the room, Tony locked his eyes on her and tracked her across the room. The Roman smiled back at Tony as she continued her graceful walk towards the challenge winner.

"Congratulations Mr. Spelling. Please come with me," she said softly, extending a hand out to the night's challenge winner. Spelling smiled and graciously took the goddess' hand. Together the pair disappeared through the same door that the Roman had originally appeared.

"What the hell is this?" questioned Tony as he looked at Mr. Y, then towards the sarcophagus, only to see the shiny grail firmly placed back on top of the stoic coffin. "I want some answers," he continued.

"Just because Mr. Spelling completed the task, doesn't mean that you get a free pass Mr. Blackwell. Are you ready Tony?" continued the host with an air of arrogance, clearly demonstrating he was in charge of the night's events.

"Bring it on you freak!" yelled Tony as he confidently stepped to the front of the platform. "If Spelling can do it, so can I," he continued while firmly grasping the shotgun in both hands.

"I am really glad to see your enthusiasm Mr. Blackwell. Ready, set, go!" commanded the night's host as Mr. Y started the stopwatch again.

Tony closed his eyes, not wanting to face his greatest fears. Instantly, the pit floor crawled with snakes of all types, colors, and sizes. The reptiles slithered over each other as if jockeying for position on top of the heap. The ceiling and walls were laden with spiders, many slowly moving, creating a moving cell of terrifying arthropods. Tony cringed as he opened his eyes to take in the terrifying room. He recognized many of the venomous snakes in the pit, from Boas, Cobras, Rattlesnakes, and Vipers to the deadly Eastern Green Mamba from Africa.

In a panic, Tony fired a round from the shotgun directly into the pool of snakes below, clearing a small path. As one minute was a short amount of time, he leapt into the small open spot, still surrounded by deadly slithering creatures. Sensing Tony's movement, a large clutter of spiders began to drop from the ceiling, several landing on Tony's head and shoulders. Many other arthropods, including Wolf, Brown Recluse, Southern Black Widow and Huntsman-Housekeeping spiders followed in a rapid repel of silk spun from each spider spinneret.

"Dammit!" yelled Tony as he frantically tried to brush the leggy creatures off his body with his left hand. His right firmly grasped the shotgun's stock. As the snakes started to invade his small opening, he fired a second shot about five feet ahead, clearing another free space. Tony raced forward to the new clearing spot, stepping directly on several thick, slimy snakes along the way. An aggressive Rattlesnake snapped at Tony's leg as his space was temporarily invaded.

"Shit!" gasped Tony. Spiders continued to fall and repel from the ceiling on and around him. Frantically, Tony fired a third shot directly at the ceiling in an attempt to quell the now constant repel of spiders. Panic set in his eyes as he realized he had not yet reached the sarcophagus and was out of ammunition.

"Throw me another shell!" he commanded towards Mr. Y, who only stared at him while he simultaneously watched the seconds tick away on the miniature chronometer in his hand.

The snakes in the pit began to wrap themselves around Tony's ankles as large numbers of spiders continued their attack from above. In a panic, Tony dropped the shotgun as he called out for help, all while swiping spiders off his shirt and running in place to free his ankles from the slithering danger around him.

Tony broke into a run towards the sarcophagus and the grail, slipping and sliding as he put each foot down on a moving slick of dangerous snakes. A pair of King Cobras rose and flared their hoods as Tony passed by. Blackwell reached the end of the pit, climbed up the small wall and grabbed the gold chalice on top of the Egyptian coffin. Knowing he was short on time, Tony turned to re-enter the snake pit.

He jumped back into the snake-filled pit and began to run as fast as he could towards the finish line. *I am going to make it,* he thought as he struggled to keep on his feet. Midway through the obstacle course, Tony slipped and fell forwards into a trove of Vipers and Pythons. He attempted to brace his fall with his hands, but they gave way as they plunged into the slithering stack of snakes. Tony's worst fear was confirmed as he now lay on top of the agitated group of arthropods. Spiders continued to drop from above and slowly began to cover his entire body.

Not giving up, Tony stood and continued his mad dash towards the finish line with the grail in tow. Spiders continued to crawl up his back and shoulders as he raced towards the end of the pit. Upon reaching the inside wall, Tony extended his arm with the grail firmly in his hand across the finish line.

Mr. Y clicked the stopwatch and looked at the face of his analog companion. "Sixty-seven seconds Mr. Blackwell," he stated with an expressionless stare. "You fail." *Snap.*

7 – WHY ME?

Tony instantly sat up in bed as he awoke from the second consecutive odd dream in the same number of nights. His breathing was heavy and he was drenched in sweat. He inhaled and exhaled slowly in an attempt to slow his racing heart.

"Are you alright?" asked Melissa, now also awake.

"No. I just had the strangest dream of my life," sighed Tony as he pulled his legs up to a sitting position.

"Another one of those work dreams?" Melissa gently reached out and stroked the wet hair out of his face.

"No," replied Tony. "This one was different." Tony started to explain the bizarre circumstances and characters associated with his now repeating dreams. His mind raced with questions. *Who is Alison Watson? Who in the hell is Mr. Y? What happened to Spelling? What the hell am I doing in this nightmare?*

"Tony, tell me what is happening," softly commanded Melissa with a concerned expression on her face.

"What I am about to tell you may seem ridiculous, but it is real to me," stated Tony as he leaned back into the bed's fluffy pillows. He pulled the down comforter over his chest as he slouched back into a defensive, but restful position, knees angled upwards making a tent within the soft protective comforter. He told Melissa the details about Mr. Y and the Egyptian challenges. When Tony was done, Melissa simply stared at him, not knowing how to react.

"This is because you are working too hard Tony," she stated. "Nothing more," she calmly continued.

"Melissa, this is *real*! I am not making this stuff up. I can see and touch things as if they are real. Please believe me!" he panted as if asking a psychologist for acceptance of his forged story.

"Forget about it Tony. They are just dreams," said Melissa. Inside, she was worried, but she didn't want Tony to know it.

* * *

Anatoly Sizy sat in his hotel room, a mere half a mile from his recent mark's home. It was morning in Georgia and the sun was shining. He listened intensely to the person on the other side of the line, taking notes on a flip-style notepad in Cyrillic with his free hand.

" Да, я понимаю," he stated in mother Russia's tongue, then disconnected the call on the mobile burner phone. "Yes, I understand," he repeated now in English. Anatoly moved to the desk and opened his laptop, which was already running a custom SVR program that communicated with the wireless device swallowed by the most recent target mark. The system options were all in Russian, but surprisingly easy to use. Agent Sizy selected the disable option and clicked the confirmation button. It was done.

The clear gelatin electronic device inside Rich Spelling was deactivated and would release from the inside walls of his intestines and dissolve in a matter of hours. Sizy closed the laptop and used the express checkout option on the television. All of the charges for his room, phone, and flight back to Moscow would hit a credit card registered to a Mr. Wilson Johnson, a Georgian native.

Anatoly reached into a black bag on the bed and retrieved an encrypted satellite phone. He dialed a number he had committed to memory long ago.

"Yes Mr. Johnson?" answered a woman.

"It is done. I am on my way back to my mother's house via Athens," he replied. Even though the call was encrypted, Sizy didn't trust the prying eyes and ears of the United State's National Security Agency, who may very well have broken Russian's rotating encryption algorithm. The line went dead.

Sizy tossed his laptop and satellite phone into the bag and zipped it closed. Ten minutes later, after wiping down the room, he exited the hotel for his trip home. After reaching the airport and prior to the security screening area, Anatoly dropped the recently purchased mobile burner phone into the trash and continued walking towards the security section. If all went well, he would never return to Georgia.

8 – ALL AROUND THE WORLD

Half way around the world and what seemed miles above Tokyo, Japan, Mr. Y had just concluded presiding over another series of dream challenges. *Three more contestants, three more failed attempts*, he thought before proclaiming victory in his own demented way.

"We have no winners tonight," he explained with his arms stretched high as if Moses calls to the Lord. The three contestants, all Asian, stood with their heads hung low, dejected that none of them had completed their challenge. Unlike other challenges Mr. Y had presided over, the unsuccessful challengers remained in the dream until the challenge was officially deemed over by the host.

The particular challenge was to shoot an arrow through various gusts of wind and burst of fire in an enclosed steel room twenty-five yards long. Large fans mounted at all corners, high and low, blew heavy winds intended to distract flying arrows from their targets. Each contestant received three arrows and professional compound bows. The missed arrows, different colors assigned to each challenger, hung in disgrace on the wall around the red circular target. The lonely female in the group dropped her bow to the floor, brought her hands to her face, and began to cry.

"Ms. Lee," called Mr. Y. "This is your last night and unfortunately, you have failed all of your challenges this week."

"Screw you!" yelled Lee as she continued to cry even louder. "I just want to go home," she whimpered, as she collapsed to her knees on the cold steel floor.

Smiling, Mr. Y snapped his fingers and instantly Ms. Lee was transported to her real life again. Lee was lying on a sterile hospital table with operating room lights blaring down on her. The tone of the heart monitor machine filled the room. It was constant and without a pulse.

"She is gone," called out one of the doctors in the room. "We did everything we could," he continued, head hung low. Losing a patient was never a good day in the life of a physician.

'What do you mean we did everything we could?" barked the senior doctor in charge still leaning over the corpse. "We don't even know what the hell she had!" he yelled as he yanked off his mask and moved away from the table in disgust.

"3:21 a.m. is the time of death," reported the head nurse in the room. "Call it."

"3:21 a.m.," repeated the youngest doctor in the room, staring straight at the clock hung on the wall. "God help us," he murmured as he switched off the heart machine, silencing the annoying steady siren. "God help us all."

The head physician retreated to his office shortly after the tumultuous session in the operating room. Internal bleeding without a known cause had taken the young woman's life. All of the blood tests searching for an infectious disease had come up empty. Dr. Tukahari paused as he sunk into his black leather chair. A dim light shone over scattered paperwork and neatly placed folders on his desk. He reached for the phone and began to dial a phone number in Atlanta, Georgia.

* * *

Melissa, with a worry on her face, jumped out of bed and headed into the kitchen to get Tony something to drink. "Orange juice ok?" she called out.

"Thanks M," replied Tony, still sitting in bed. His heart rate and breathing now under control. "What the hell is happening to me Melissa?

"You just had a bad dream sweetie. Don't worry about it," she said in a calming voice as she returned from the kitchen and handed Tony a fresh glass of juice. "This work project of yours is stressing you out way too much."

"You don't understand M. This isn't the first time I've had one of these," he stated in between gulps. "These are really messed up," he continued. Melissa sat down on the bed next to him, seeming to settle in for a long story. Tony began to talk about Mr. Y again. "He runs the show and we are all competing in these weird challenges while we dream. They change each night and sometimes there are new people competing. One guy succeeded in a challenge and he was whisked away by this Roman goddess," he continued.

"You have got to be kidding me," laughed Melissa as she sipped from her own glass of orange juice. "If you have Roman goddesses in your dreams, they can't be all that bad," she joked. "They are just dreams, nothing more."

"I am serious Melissa. I had two of these fucking dreams in a row and in each of them, I am asked to do something that is damn near impossible as this ancient philosopher host named Mr. Y looks on and times us," continued Tony. "He hovers too."

"Hovers?"

"Yes. Mr. Y doesn't have any feet and just hovers. He can also snap things into place at will. He creates the challenges, changes the obstacles, selects the weapons, and can change the makeup of any room we are in with the snap of his fingers. The Egyptian snake pit was really creepy. I could also feel the spiders biting me on my back and shoulders. Do I have any bites on my back?"

Melissa smiled as she stroked his cheek with her hand. "Just dreams." Tony turned around in the bed to show Melissa his back. Several small bite marks adorned his upper back and neck. Melissa was horrified. *How is this possible?* she thought.

"These are different Melissa. For some reason, I feel different after each dream, like I am getting weaker or older," continued Tony. "Do I have any bite marks?"

"Just a few bites, likely from a mosquito," returned Melissa.

"Melissa, I did *not* have them yesterday. How is that possible? My legs ache with a deep-level pain," he continued as he started to massage his cramped quadriceps. Tony repeated the details of his two recent dreams. He explained every contest and rule put in place by the mysterious host. When he finished, Tony got out of bed exasperated and headed into the bathroom. "So, explain that Melissa?" he called out from the bathroom, slamming the door behind him.

"M, something's not right about this, but I don't know what it is," called out Tony from inside the bathroom. He placed both hands on the rim of the sink and looked into the mirror intently at his mirror image. "God, please do not let me dream tonight," he spoke softly, never blinking. "Not tonight."

* * *

Anya Kuzma looked at the image on her laptop. The screen blinked in the lower right-hand section with the Russian phrase прекращено. Her mark was *terminated*. Her work on the target was almost done. A report was due to her handler in Tokyo within three hours. Where it would go from there she did not know. After the report was sent, she would go to ground until she received her next assignment.

9 – BACK TO WORK

Melissa and Tony stepped out of the apartment complex and headed to work. It was 7:45 a.m. and both had important meetings. Melissa's meeting with the vice principal of her school was to discuss her performance for the quarter. Most of the staff thought that she was a good teacher and one who clearly loved being around the children in her fourth grade class. The pair walked the sidewalk hand in hand on their way to the T subway station.

"Listen Tony, you've got to let this dream stuff go. I am sure it is totally stress related and that you will get over it soon," continued Melissa as she swung his hand in hers backwards and forwards. Tony remained silent. Two dreams in two nights and he was starting to worry about what was happening to him physically and mentally.

"My legs are cramping up M," he said as he stopped their brisk walk and reached down to rub his sore muscles. "What the hell is happening to me?" he whispered to himself.

"What honey?" asked Melissa.

"Nothing. Nothing at all," he replied. "I am fine," stated Tony as he resumed their walk.

After Tony purchased subway tokens, the couple paused before parting ways, each headed in different directions. Melissa reached up to give Tony a kiss. "Try and have a good day Tony," she said.

"You too, and don't worry about me Melissa. I'll be fine," replied Tony, masking his true emotions. *Something is definitely wrong,* he thought as he kissed Melissa on the forehead.

* * *

Melissa reached the Park Elementary School and began preparing for her meeting with the vice principal. The room was filled with a host of pictures and drawings from her class as well as several educational posters appropriate for fourth grade students. The room was warm and cozy. She felt comfortable in her classroom.

"Melissa, when did you get here?" asked Ms. Russo, another fourth grade teacher. "I have been here for twenty minutes, but I didn't see you come in," she continued.

"Hi Julia," returned Melissa. "I just got in. How are you today girl?" she continued. Melissa had a good relationship with many of the teachers in the school. Julia entered the classroom and walked up to give Melissa a hug.

"I have my meeting with the boss today too, about thirty minutes after yours," she replied.

"Oh Julia, you will do just fine today," replied Melissa. "You are one of the best teachers in this school," she continued.

"You are so sweet young lady. So, how is it going? Are you ready for the meeting?"

"Of course, but I have a couple of things on my mind," continued Melissa.

"Like what?" returned Julia as she sat down in one of the available chairs.

"Oh, nothing here," she returned. "My boyfriend Tony – you remember him?" she continued.

"Sure. He is a keeper," reflected Julia as a smile appeared on her face.

"Oh, I know. Well, he has been having these really weird dreams and it is starting to freak him out," continued Melissa. "And since he started having these dreams, his leg muscles are tightening up on him. Have you ever heard of anything like that?"

"That sounds really strange," replied Julia. "But I am sure that the dreams and cramps are not related," she continued. "I mean, who gets physically ill from dreams, right? Tony is probably just coming down with something at the same time."

"I don't know, but I hope you are right my friend," replied Melissa. "Hey, I have got to get ready for my meeting with Jill. Can I catch up with you later?" she politely asked.

"Sure," replied her friend. "Do well," she concluded as she reached up to touch her friend on the shoulder. Melissa continued with her document review in preparation for her meeting twenty minutes later. Her mind, of course, was still thinking about the man she had fallen in love with.

* * *

Tony arrived at his office slightly ahead of his peers as usual. He was glad it was finally Friday. As usual, Tony was dressed meticulously, sometimes rivaling that of a Wall Street banker instead of a Boston actuary. Richie stopped by to get his trusted colleagues' input on another project. Tony's crisp dark blue pinstripe suit matched with a signature series silk tie from Milan drew the attention of other women in the office as he made his way to his cube. In short – Tony looked like a cover boy from *GQ* magazine, but did not carry the typical arrogance of a model.

"Hey buddy, do you have some time to work on the Redstone project?" asked Richie, just as Tony began to settle in at his desk.

"What, now?"

"If not now, when?" replied Richie as he move in to take a glance at Tony's calendar for an opening.

"Ok, ok. Let's get this over now so I can focus on the rest of my day." Tony bumped Richie's arm as he reached down to use his computer keyboard to block off thirty minutes on his calendar. "Ugh," he continued while reaching for his iPhone, which was now buzzing to indicate new email messages. Tony glanced at the small screen and efficiently maneuvered the device to reply to one of the messages as he stood up and started walking down the hallway. "You coming?" he stated without even looking up from the smart phone.

"Yeah man. Thanks" The two strolled down the hall. Richie paused at his desk to collect a folder with notes and research before increasing his pace to catch up with his friend and co-worker.

"Katie, please block off conference room 21B for forty-five minutes," stated Tony into his mobile phone. Katie was on speed dial for obvious reasons and Tony leveraged her often to coordinate meetings with clients and co-workers. The two strode into the room, closed the door, and got to work. Even though the Redstone project was not Tony's responsibility, he was happy to help his friend. Everyone in the office knew that Tony was a rising star and he knew too well that sharing knowledge and helping others would help him rise even faster through the ranks of management.

* * *

"Melissa. To close this quarterly review, you are such an asset to the Park Street School and we're so happy to have you," stated Dr. Hillen.

"Thank you Jill," replied Melissa casually and humbly, feeling comfortable enough to call the senior educator by her first name. "I am really fortunate to be here and learn from folks like you and the other more senior teachers."

"Well, I look forward to many more solid semesters from you. Keep up the great work Melissa," replied Jill as she stood up and extended her hand to congratulate the young and talented teacher.

Melissa walked out of the principal's office and towards the classroom that she had become to know as her daytime home.

She smiled. The day progressed for each of the two young lovers.

* * *

The day ended with progress. Tony had completed all of his assignments. "Hey Tony. We've got to get out of here," called Richie from down the hall. "Time for racquetball buddy," he continued as he collected his papers to read for the weekend, stuffing them into his briefcase rapidly and randomly. The pair headed out of the office complex with many others at the end of their busy day. The elevators seemed unusually crowded at this time of the day, but it was Friday.

Many of the young professionals at the bank were either heading out to happy hour or to hit the gym. Some, especially the upwardly mobile, would no doubt return to the office and continue into the early night. The two reached the street and started to walk east two blocks towards the sports complex. In Boston, everything was convenient. The gym where he and most of his friends worked out was conveniently tucked inside one of the beautiful sky liners in the city. Tony loved living in Boston.

"Hey Richie. I think I've got the research that Roberts may think twice about," he stated as the pair walked briskly up the stairs towards the gym's entrance.

"You still thinking about that asshole? Give it up man. He'll never let you succeed because he is concerned about you taking his job someday."

"That's ridiculous. I am just trying to do my best job for the bank. Man, I hate these stupid office politics," continued Tony as he swiped his gym badge through the scanner that served as the electronic gatekeeper to the gym. *Thank God for technology*, he thought. If it were not for supercomputers and programming languages, he could not do his job effectively. They crunched numbers and algorithms that Tony created to look for better profit margins.

The pair headed into the locker room to change for their weekly battle on the court. Each was respectful of the other's intellect, but on the racquetball court – it was all out war. The winner had bragging rights for the entire week. The pair arrived at court three with goggles, gloves, and rackets ready to duel.

Richie started to hit successive practice balls into the far wall with precision and skill, while Tony began to stretch against the front wall near the narrow entrance door. Five forehands followed by five backhands, each bounced twenty-four or so inches above the floor before Richie repeated the series. Both young men were quite skilled at the fast court game that required an understanding of mathematics, angle precision, and raw speed. Richie soon became bored with his one-on-one exercise.

"What the hell are you doing old man?"

"Sorry," replied Tony as he slowly moved to the center of the backcourt ready to receive his friend's serve. He rubbed his right calve with his free hand, trying to loosen the tight muscles that were causing him obvious pain. "I've been really sore lately and now my forearms are really tight," he continued.

"Shut up already Father Time. Let's go! You ready?"

"Fire away," replied Tony. His eyes now focused on the wall ahead. Tony settled into a split step and somewhat crouched, ready position, slightly rocking side to side on the balls of his feet in anticipation. Richie fired a precise serve to the far left corner. Tony instinctively moved away from the back wall to anticipate the bounce and fired a backhand shot directly at the front left wall. The blue rubber ball hugged the side wall as it whistled towards its target and slammed into the wall, five inches from the floor leaving Richie with his first service loss.

"Whoa! I didn't see that coming Superman," stated Richie jokingly while conceding the point and switching places with Tony in the defensive part of the court. Tony humbly walked toward the service box and bounced the ball four times with his left hand while facing the opposite side wall in a classic service stance.

"Ready?"

"Bring it," snapped Richie.

The pair proceeded with their mini-war on the court. Each gave it their all in the hardwood sports theater. An occasional ace and diving save were commonplace in their matches. Sweat poured down each of their faces as the match went forward, each point becoming more intense than the prior one. After an hour and four long games, Tony as usual, was the victor, winning three of the four games.

"Dude, what got into you today?" said the loser.

"Sorry. Just thinking about a lot of stuff these days my friend and I needed an outlet," replied Tony.

"Don't apologize for beating me man. I can see your mind is elsewhere. I'm not a total idiot you know."

The two shook hands and headed towards the showers. Tony placed a hand on his trusted friend's shoulder as the pair exited the small door leading to the open weight room section of the gym. "Hey, what do you know about dreams?" he cautiously stated.

"All I know is that the best ones I've ever had involved a Scorpion Bowl from the Hong Kong, a hot chick, and a happy ending," replied Richie with a huge smile on his face.

"I thought so. Never mind." Once showered, the men hit the street. Their gym bags, with work clothes folded nicely inside, dangled from their shoulders like man-purses. Tony pulled his cell phone out of the side pocket from his Adidas bag and placed a call to Melissa.

"Hey, we're done. What are you doing tonight?"

"I'm heading over to Mary's tonight for dinner and a few drinks. You know, she's the fifth grade teacher I keep telling you about," replied Melissa.

"Yeah, I remember. Listen, sorry about tonight. I just have to get my head together about this revised presentation to Tom and just need some time to think clearly. If you're interested, stop by my place after drinks."

"I'd love to sweetie, but I'm going to let you have your time tonight. Something tells me that your mind won't be on me and you know how I get when I'm not the center of attention with you," she said jokingly.

"I'm sorry. I'll call you in the morning."

"Good luck tonight."

"Thanks and M – I love you," replied Tony after a brief pause.

"I adore you Tony Blackwell," responded Melissa. Tony smiled as he imagined her facial expression while she uttered those poetic words.

* * *

Tony had MTV playing on the television without any volume. Several lit candles provided a calming atmosphere while he worked on the presentation to the head of his division. The research that he had done was good, but not good enough. Simply put – nobody in the banking community had done what Tony had recommended. That made him feel good. He knew that he was right and could put the bank on a new course of improved profitability in the coming year if he was just given a chance. *You have to deliver the sale to Roberts*, he thought while he refined a complex two-dimensional bar chart.

The evening progressed and Tony continued to make progress. He took several breaks, listened to the stereo and switched the channel to watch CNBC in between working sessions. Three quarters of a pizza and two Cokes later, he settled in for a long night of studying and preparation. As 1 a.m. approached, he was still at it. Red Sox pajama bottoms and a bare chest accompanied the lone candle still burning on the side table. As Tony stared at the PowerPoint presentation on his laptop. His eyes blinked several times, noticeably slower. He was beyond tired. "Please don't let me fall asleep," he muttered. Seconds later, his eyes fell shut and his hands went limp on the keyboard. He had lost the battle of consciousness to the demon that was about to come from inside him.

* * *

Anastasia Minkin had just delivered the package to the unsuspecting Canadian female. She finished deploying the communications uplink when she received an encrypted message on her custom smart phone.

Message: Implement task 7T and report back in twenty-four hours. - Sasha.

She read and deleted the message before moving back to her rental car. The late model Jeep blended in with the others in the Snow Belt area. Minkin turned on the engine and flipped the heater on full fan. She opened her laptop, moved the mouse to the appropriate position on the screen, and activated the device. After the program received the signal, the screen blinked green twice and updated the status indicator. Anastasia paused, smiled, and closed her computer. Moments later, she pulled the gear handle into automatic and drove off.

10 - A RACE WITH THE Y

Alison Watson stood on a desolate road next to Tony and a new contestant. Rich Spelling was out and a new woman was in the game. Tony looked first at Alison, then at the new woman. She was older, mid-forties or so and on the plump side. As Tony sized her up, he wondered how she could possibly succeed. *She doesn't look athletic at all*. But then again – he had yet to win a challenge even given his natural sporting ability.

"Alison. It's great to see you again," said Tony awkwardly as he walked towards the blond beauty. He could not take his eyes off her. She was breathtaking.

"Tony, right?"

"Yeah. Sixth time, right?" Alison smiled. Her smile was warm and genuine, exposing the subtle dimples on her cheeks. She was dressed in a pair of white Capri pants, a royal blue golf shirt, and open shoe sandals, exposing her matching painted toenails. She had the body of a finely tuned athlete, combined with the look of a swimsuit model. Silver hoop earrings hung from her lobes as they shimmered in the sunlight. Tony looked closer and could see her underwear lines and color peeking through the thinly lined white fabric.

"God, you're beautiful," blurted Tony, almost wishing that he had not uttered the words as soon as he spoke them.

"What did you say?

"I'm sorry," he replied, hanging his head slightly with eyes still focused on her. His heart was racing faster now. *Who is this woman?* he thought to himself. *Where is she from?* He wanted to know much more about her. "I didn't think before I," stated Tony.

"It is ok," she replied as she took his hand into hers. "You're cute and sweet," she continued. "You're the only thing in these weird contests that doesn't make me sick," she continued.

"Right," sighed Tony as he let his grip on her hand go limp.

"No, no. I didn't mean it like that."

"I know," he replied with a warm smile, now re-grasping her hand. Their eyes met and each was speechless for a brief moment.

"Contests, right? Do you think anyone else is watching these and we can't see them?"

"I do not know, but I wouldn't be surprised."

"Ok lovebirds," interrupted Mr. Y, now hovering near a group of three exotic sports cars parked in a line perpendicular to an all too familiar white line crossing the road. All three contestants looked at Mr. Y, then at the cars, trying to anticipate what the challenge would be. Alison let go of Tony's hand as she stared in amazement at the vehicles. Sand and dirt whipped across the lonely road as the grains danced inside small invisible cyclones. Nothing else was around. Just the four, three contestants and Mr. Y, standing in the middle of nowhere. No other cars, people or activity were anywhere in sight. A mountain draped in a blanket of snow was visible all around. Tony broke away from the others to take in his surroundings as he moved towards the cars. He recognized the place, but where was it? Where had he seen it before? In a movie? On a post card? Where?

"I need a volunteer tonight. Any takers?" boldly stated the now infamous host.

"For what?" responded the new candidate, clearly looking like the freshman of the group.

"Welcome Ms. Holloway. Ah, this is your first attempt, yes?"

"Attempt at what?" questioned the middle-aged woman, articulating her words in a clear Canadian accent. Clearly, more tense and uptight than the others, she fidgeted while standing and seemed to look around at her surroundings with angst. Her appearance clashed with her non-fashionable attire – baggy blue jeans with a tee shirt that was clearly too big for her frame. She dressed as if she was trying to conceal her extra weight.

"I am Mr. Y and your host tonight," continued the magical man. The gray in his beard sparkled against the sun that fully shined on his face. "Tonight, we race. You each may select from one of the cars in front of you. Once the light turns green, you have two minutes to race to the end of the road and return here to cross this line," he stated, pointing to the white line in the middle of the road. Two towers instantly appeared on each side of the road. Both towers contained a series of vertically mounted lights, five in total per side.

"A drag race," muttered Tony. "I will take the," he started in anticipation.

"Not your turn yet Blackwell," interrupted Mr. Y. "I pick the order tonight. You pick the cars, starting with you Tara," he continued, gazing into the eyes of the confused Canadian.

"Me? Why me? I've never driven one of those things before," she huffed in frustration.

"Next is Alison, then Tony. That is the order tonight."

"I want the Porsche 911 turbo," called out Tony.

"Tara?" asked the host politely. "Time is ticking," he joked as he held up the stopwatch in his hand.

"Dear Lord. I'll take the red one."

"The Audi R8. An excellent choice." Mr. Y snapped his fingers and in an instant, Tara Holloway was sitting in the driver's seat of the bright red super car, positioned directly in front of the two light towers. Mr. Y was sitting in a gloss white Lamborghini Murcielago convertible, tricked out with white alloy rims wrapped inside high performance low profile black racing tires. Both cars were running, each politely coughing small puffs of smoke out their exhaust while the engines rumbled in idle. Mr. Y pressed the accelerator and the Murcielago came to life with a high-pitched roar, distinctive only to the Lamborghini Italian luxury car.

"I have a special treat for you Tara," he said calmly from within a black-smoked windscreen lifted up from his white helmet. She could hear him clearly even through the sound of the car's engines. Her helmet was connected via a two-way wireless intercom directly to the host.

"What?" clearly hearing him, but not understanding.

"When you reach the end of the road and start your turn back, I will pick another machine that you have a fear of driving," he smiled while looking directly at her. Tony and Melissa could not hear the conversation and stood to the side, wondering what was about to happen.

"And yes, I know what the other machine is," he smiled. "Ready?" stopwatch poised in his left hand while his right was clutching the steering wheel.

"No!" screamed Tara. The lights on the tower started to flash from top to bottom, starting first in red. The blinking was accompanied by a loud beeping sound at each light with just enough of a pause between each light to mesmerize the drivers. The synchronous light show and countdown continued. Five, four, three, two, continued the countdown. The last light at the bottom turned green.

The two cars accelerated off the starting line. The Lamborghini laid a screeching patch that swirled smoke off the black asphalt. Tara pushed the gas pedal to the floor and squeezed the steering wheel as if she was holding onto the safety railing of a terrifying rollercoaster, both hands on the top. Mr. Y had a clear lead with a near perfect start, but Tara gained on him as the car automatically shifted through the gears, rapidly gaining speed.

"That's right," smirked the seemingly insane host. "Keep coming," he continued as he flirted with her, intentionally easing up on the accelerator and drawing her in. The message was selectively blocked and not delivered to Tara's helmet. Tara increased her speed to one hundred and thirty miles per hour. She moved the Audi to the four o'clock position behind the sleek Lamborghini. Fifty-five seconds into the race and the pair were side by side. Mr. Y looked towards his competitor and started to slow his sports machine, downshifting to fourth, then third, anticipating the one hundred and eighty degree turn before lunging into the second half of the challenge. As he did so, Tara followed, shifting into third gear while depressing the brakes. The car lurched slightly forward as the engine roared above five thousand RPMs.

"Ready for the return run?" called the host.

"Stop!" replied the increasingly terrified racer. As the pair passed the bright red cone in the center of the road, led first by Mr. Y, then his challenger, the mysterious host snapped his fingers. Quickly shifting into second gear, he slammed the accelerator to the floor, causing the white rocket to jump forward while slightly spinning out of control to the right side.

"Whoa!" called out the host. "What a rush." Tara followed in pursuit and remembered what the host said to her at the starting line. She closed her eyes and started to scream. When she opened her eyes, she was driving a cigarette speedboat, hair flapping in the breeze in a water channel that did not exist just seconds before. The narrow waterway ran directly parallel to the desert road. *An inlet in the middle of the desert*, she thought.

"How in the hell?" she called out into the front wind that swallowed her voice. Instinctively however, she grabbed hold of the sleek fiberglass's wheel and slammed the silver throttle to her right forward. The engines reared up and the boat's front rose off the horizon as it started to pick up speed. She was well behind her host now and losing ground. *How can I catch him?* she thought.

The boat continued to increase speed until it reached eighty miles per hour. At that speed, Tara became very nervous. The boat was much more difficult to keep straight in the narrow channel as it neared its top speed. Tara's eyes were now fully squinted, with tears streaming down her face as she tried to focus on the path ahead without a helmet or goggles to protect her vision. Mr. Y shifted into sixth gear and the Lamborghini sped towards one hundred and fifty miles per hour.

Tara could see the sports car getting more and more out of reach. The finish line was ahead, but she knew she could not close the gap in time to cross the line ahead of Mr. Y. Seconds later, the white Lamborghini ripped through a white tape banner imprinted with "winner," positioned over top of the white line painted onto the road. Mr. Y jerked the steering wheel to the left, causing the car to slide sideways at a forty-five degree angle to the road. Moments later the car came to a stop. A plume of white smoke created by burning rubber dragged along the asphalt passed the car moments later. Mr. Y sighed with satisfaction. Seeing the glorious finish by her host, Ms. Holloway pulled back on the super-boat's throttle and accepted defeat. The forty-five foot cigarette boat slowed instantly and crossed the line with its wake pushing water to either side of the bow. Tara stopped the gurgling twin engines and the boat slowly drifted to a near stop.

Mr. Y removed his white helmet, placed it in the passenger seat, and began to levitate out of the car, floating upwards until he was again hovering near the other contestants. "Let's see. I crossed the line in one minute, fifty seconds flat and you Ms. Holloway, drifted across the finish line in two minutes and eleven seconds. Thus, you fail," he continued. The amused host could see the tears welling up in the poor woman's eyes. Before they could complete their staggered journey down her cheek, he snapped his fingers, causing Tara to freeze all motion. Even the tears stopped their fall across her rosy cheeks. Two claps later and she disappeared completely. The contestant and car was removed from sight.

Tony and Alison just stared at the space once occupied by their co-challenger. "If my memory is correct," stated the host. "Ms. Watson, you are next."

"Don't do it Alison!" barked Tony. "Seriously, what if we turn the tables on this thing and just don't participate? He can't make us, can he?"

"Actually, young Tony is correct," responded Mr. Y. "You don't have to participate," he continued.

"Let's just walk the hell out of here towards those mountains and see what's on the other side," continued Tony, his imagination now running wild. "I bet there are other people that can help us," he continued as he reached for Alison's hand and attempted to pull her away from the latest challenge."

"I'm not sure Tony," replied Alison.

"Actually, it's not that simple Mr. Blackwell, but nice try," responded the host. "See, if you fail to participate, then you fail the challenge. It's really just that simple," a smile returned to his face.

"Alison! Listen. Let's get the hell out of here," pleaded Tony.

"No. I'm going to try and beat him," returned the blond beauty.

"That's the spirit," shot back Mr. Y. "I see you've picked the Aston Martin Ms. Watson," continued the host.

"No she didn't!" yelled Tony, now looking at Alison, who was staring directly at the host.

"That's exactly what she just did."

"I'm sorry Tony. It just popped into my head," she said. "I can beat him. Trust me," she whispered towards Tony. She placed her hands on either side of Tony's face and stared into his eyes. "I can beat him," she mouthed.

"Then, it is show time!" called the host, snapping his fingers. Instantly the sleek steel-gray Aston Martin was sitting on the starting line – again next to the Lamborghini, both running and rumbling. Alison kissed Tony on the cheek.

"I'll be right back," she stated confidently. As Alison pulled away from him, Tony reached out for her hand, but it was too late. She was walking with intent towards the sports car. Alison opened the passenger door and reached for the helmet, clearly looking like a woman on a mission. After putting on the protective gear and adjusting the chin strap, she slammed the passenger door shut and familiarized herself with the car. Alison revved the engine and glanced over to her competitor, who was already in his seat and chomping at the bit for a fight. The intense stare between the two was not long, and only broken when Alison flipped her helmet's eye shield down.

"I have a special treat for you Alison," repeated Mr. Y for the second contestant of the night.

"What do you want?" replied Alison, clearly forecasting her impatience.

"When you reach the end of the road and start your turn back, your beautiful Aston Martin will be replaced by a machine that you have a fear of driving," replied Mr. Y. "Are you ready?"

Alison did not even flinch and assumed that whatever popped into her mind had eluded her host. It did not.

"Let's go you freak," she whispered softly into the built-in microphone as she revved her engine multiple times. Tony watched from afar and crossed his fingers behind his back with anticipation. The lights on the tower started again from top to bottom, first in red. Five, four, three, two, one! The two cars lurched off the line in near even precision. Alison slammed the gas pedal to the floor and the car did the rest, as she was driving in automatic mode. Ten seconds into the race, both cars were dead even with one another and accelerating at tremendous speeds. Mr. Y smiled as he acknowledged her driving skills. He was not pulling back this time. To him, win or lose was irrelevant. Alison would only win if she crossed the line before the two-minute mark.

"Not bad," communicated the host as the pair crossed one hundred miles per hour. Alison did not respond, instead focused on the task of winning the race. Fifty seconds into the race and nearing the turn, Alison maintained a slight lead. The engines screamed as they continued to push harder on the desolate road. As Mr. Y started to downshift in preparation for his turn, Alison maintained pace, somewhat confusing her host. Mr. Y dropped the Lamborghini into third, slowing the white monster and losing more ground to his female competitor.

Alison instead waited one more second before slamming on the brakes, causing Mr. Y to swerve to avoid a collision with the back of the DB9. Looking in her rear-view mirror, she smiled as she had lured in and confused her prey. Still breaking, her car slowed more rapidly than Mr. Y's and as a result, it got her closer to the turn. Mr. Y hit the brakes and dropped to second gear before he punched the accelerator and followed the leader out of the turn.

"Yahoo!" yelled Alison as she rounded the corner in the lead.

"Ready?" called the host.

"Oh no!" replied the shocked racer, forgetting for a moment that she wouldn't be driving the sports car that she'd become comfortable with back to the finish line. Mr. Y snapped his fingers. By the time Alison had blinked, she was now in the cockpit of a U.S. Navy F/A-18 fighter jet.

"Goddammit!" shouted Alison. She was not fond of airplanes, let alone warplanes. She avoided planes whenever possible in her real life. The plane was in full motion, flying at well over a hundred and sixty miles per hour, only a few feet above the dusty ground. "Come on Casey, give me strength," she muttered to herself, reminiscent of her childhood friend who died in a commercial airline accident just a few years ago.

Alison hastily grabbed hold of the flight stick between her legs, and rotated the throttle, causing the jet to accelerate as it came out of the turn. The twin-engines responded with a roar, creating a mini-vortex of dust and smoke behind her. Wearing full flight gear with an oxygen mask dangling to the side of her helmet, she glanced down to search for the Lamborghini.

"Son-of-a-bitch. No you don't," she blurted, noticing that her slight navigational error had placed her off-course and farther away from the road. Mr. Y continued to accelerate as he headed for the home stretch towards the finish line. A trail of dust was clearly visible behind the white ground missile as the car sped towards the finish line.

Using the fighter jet's rudders to control the aircraft left and right while guiding the stick, she maneuvered the plane towards the finish line, approaching it from a thirty-degree angle to the right of the road. The split tail jet engines burned a steady stream of yellow fire from the back of the sleek gray war bird as the plane accelerated to close the gap with the super car below. Alison began to count aloud as the jet, now twenty feet above the ground, closed in on the target.

"Ten, nine, eight, seven." Mr. Y and the Lamborghini passed through one hundred and seventy miles an hour, running a near flawless second leg of the race. "Three, two," continued Alison as the jet roared overhead of the elite white car and passed over the finish line a plane length before her host.

"One, mother fucker!" she concluded as she pulled back on the stick, causing the jet to ascend straight up into the sky. Using the ailerons expertly, the plane spun in precision as it pierced into the darkening blue sky above, still climbing. "Wahoo!" she called into the microphone after latching the oxygen mask securely in place over her mouth.

Mr. Y slowed his car to an eventual stop and clapped his hands, applauding the contestant's test. "Nice job Ms. Watson. Nice job indeed." Alison completed her spinning climb, straightened the aircraft so that it was horizontal with the ground for a moment as the win sunk in. She then snapped the stick to the right and forward, forcing the aircraft into a dive, leaving the opposite side of the finish banner visible ahead of her. As she approached the ground at well over five hundred miles an hour, the warplane buzzed directly over Tony and Mr. Y, smiling as she did so. After being satisfied with her fly-by, she landed the plane squarely on the road and coasted the aircraft, engines now winding down, to stop directly in front of the finish line.

"Congratulations Ms. Watson," stated the host. "Not only did you beat me, but you came across the line at one minute and fifty seconds."

"Yeah!" responded Alison as she climbed out of the cockpit and onto the wing, helmet still in her hand. Tony raced towards the plane to congratulate his new friend and possible love interest. As he approached the aircraft, he heard that all too familiar sound. *Snap!* Instantly Alison and the plane were gone.

"What have you done with her?" he demanded.

"Mr. Blackwell. She won," he replied with a perplexed look on his face. "She's done, gone."

"You son-of-a-bitch!" Tony sprinted towards the strange host and as he got within ten feet or so, Mr. Y held up his hand, palm up like a stop sign. Tony instantly stopped in his tracks and began to levitate a foot above the dusty tan ground. He tried to speak, but could not. Sweat started to bead on his forehead and an expression of both pain and frustration overtook his entire face.

"Mr. Blackwell. Please don't forget that it's rude to attack your host and I simply won't allow it," stated Mr. Y as he slowly moved his extended arm to the right and put Tony back onto solid land.

"You," stated Tony. Mr. Y just shook his index finger back and forth, now controlling his contestant's voice.

"Now, let's get back to our festivities, shall we? I'd say that leaves you with the red Porsche as you requested initially," continued his host, clearly in control and showing no emotion at all on his face. Tony just stared at him, trying to catch his breath and wondered how in the hell he could get near him to beat the living hell out of him.

Snap! Mr. Y was again sitting in the driver's seat of the Lamborghini, this time wearing black sunglasses that clearly contrasted with his white image, and stared directly at Tony. The red Porsche 911 Turbo sat next to the Lamborghini, awaiting its fate, which depended heavily on the driver. Tony buckled his seat belt and closed the black eye shield of his matching red helmet.

"What is it this time, Mr. Y?" called Tony. "A ship, hovercraft, huh?" mocking his host.

"You'll find out Mr. Blackwell, but I can assure you that it will be one fun trip," replied the cocky host.

"Then let's do this thing," commanded Tony as he revved the Porsche's engine.

"Before we start Mr. Blackwell, I have a special treat for you," he said calmly as he had with the other contestants, all in confidence. "When you reach the end of the road and start your turn back, I will pick another machine that you have a fear of driving," he smiled while looking directly at Tony.

"The funny thing is that I already know what that is," he laughed. Ready?"

"Yes."

The lights on the tower started to flash from top to bottom, initially in red again. *The loud blaring noise synchronized with the lights was especially annoying the third time around,* thought Tony. Three, two, one as the final light turned green. The two cars screamed off the starting line. Tony caught Mr. Y by surprise as he took a split second lead. The pair of racers continued to accelerate, each shifting manually and slightly trading on and off for the lead as they passed through fourth gear and one hundred miles per hour. Tony slammed the Porsche into fifth an instant before his competitor and the car nudged forward to take the lead. Smiling, Mr. Y responded and used the more powerful Lamborghini's six hundred and forty horse powered engine to re-take the lead.

"Time for some fun," mused Tony as he jerked the wheel left, causing the cars to bump sides. Mr. Y did not speak and seemed surprised at the move. Tony, running neck and neck with the Lamborghini as they shifted into sixth, yanked the wheel a second time. This time the Porsche scraped up against the front right side of the gloss white roadster, causing Mr. Y to briefly lose control of the car as it slid off the road. The move, kicked up a storm of dust that prevented the host from seeing which direction he was driving. Tony laughed as he hit the accelerator and pointed the car down the middle of the road, directly over the dotted white line previously separating the two racers moments ago.

"Ha, ha!" shouted Tony.

"I've got to give you some credit Mr. Blackwell," returned Mr. Y to his adversary. "I didn't say that there were any rules other than what was stated now did I?" he continued as the tires moved from the dirt to the pavement and squealed as the car regained traction as Mr. Y lit up the engine in pursuit of the red Porsche. Fifty-five seconds had passed since the race started and Tony could now see the red cone clearly, indicating that he was almost half way through the race. Blackwell downshifted to fourth, then to second, as he swung the car in anticipation of a sliding left one hundred and eighty degree turn. As he raced in second gear, Tony looked into the rear-view mirror and saw the white Lamborghini gaining on him. Rounding the corner, he punched the gas and jammed the stick forward into third gear.

Before the gears actually took hold, time paused for a second without any forward motion. Instantly, Tony was sitting inside the cockpit of a flat black AH-64 Apache helicopter, four-bladed rotor spinning above him to a synchronized thumping sound.

"What the hell?" stressed Tony as the chopper hovered just passed the red cone. Mr. Y's super car rounded the cone and started to pick up speed. Tony could hear the high-pitched sound of the accelerating Lamborghini below him, then saw the white car dart out and take the lead back to the finish line. Tony briefly looked inside the cockpit at the instruments as the attack machine hovered. Dials, LED readout, and gauges filled the cramped inside of the Apache. Sitting in the front position of the tandem-seated attack helicopter was a Marine gunner, dressed in battle gear.

"Major Blackwell. Let's go get him, sir," barked the gunner and co-pilot. Tony froze, taking in everything around him. "Sir!" called the gunner again. As Tony reached for the controls, the view of the car ahead of him went dark. Everything outside and in the killing machine lit up with an eerie green hue.

"Oh my God," blurted Tony. He was going to have to fly this thing at night. *Why did everything all of the sudden go dark?* he thought. No time to think, just fly and fly he did. He grabbed hold of the controls and the stealth aircraft leaned forward in pursuit of an adversary that Tony could no longer see without the assistance of night vision equipment. As Tony increased speed, the winds kicked up dirt and sand all around the AH-64.

Instantly, the inside windshield lit up with all kinds of symbols and objects as the Pilot Night Vision Sensor system came to life. The Apache rapidly gained speed on a now visible ground target that the helicopter was tracking electronically. Tony maneuvered the craft lower to the ground and directly in line with the center of the road, now chasing Mr. Y. Within ten seconds, he could see the Lamborghini right ahead. It appeared as an oddly shaped green triangle on the heads up display, with a variety of circles and larger triangles automatically positioned as vectors around the target. The attack chopper was gaining quickly on its prey.

"I'm going to kill that son-of-a-bitch." Tony glanced at the airspeed indicator and it was nearly static at one hundred and thirty knots. Time was running out and the super car was moving farther away from the Apache with every passing second. Tony pushed the button that activated the sixteen laser-guided Hellfire missiles.

Using his right thumb, Tony flipped open the fire safety and exposed the small red circle that controlled the primary weapons. "Fire!" he yelled as he pressed the button, still navigating. The Apache responded with a Hellfire missile that swooshed out from below the starboard wing towards the target. The green indicators on the windshield indicated that the weapon had not locked onto its target yet and within moments, the powerful missile passed the Lamborghini just to the right and struck the ground. "Shit!"

The explosion rocked the Lamborghini and upon impact, Mr. Y turned to see the exact position of the attack helicopter. His adversary had launched the rocket with lock-on-after-launch acquisition mode, which required the sophisticated computers to acquire its target after comparing it to the onboard database. *Five more seconds.* Tony, starting to panic, maneuvered the craft until he was able to lock onto the target below him before firing his weapon. A screeching sound pierced the inside of the cockpit.

"I have tone, Sergeant. Fire, fire!" yelled Tony to the gunner as he focused on flying the helicopter.

"Firing," returned the gunner. This time, the missile launched from under the port side wing of the aircraft, now slightly in a correcting bank turn. The war machine's computer system instantly started to track the weapon on the heads up display. The missile's trail of smoke was in rapid pursuit of the small car below and seemed destined to hit the target.

"Three, two, one. You're done," calmly stated Mr. Y as the Lamborghini screamed across the finish line, the missile still in hot pursuit. *Snap.*

11 – BLOODY SATURDAY

Alison opened her eyes, only to see a swarm of doctors surrounding her. She was in a sterile room with silver tables and bright fluorescent lights shining down on her.

"What just happened to me?" she whispered.

"Miss Watson. Do you know where you are?" responded one of the doctors leaning over her. Her eyes fell shut again, causing the doctors to scramble.

"We're losing her again Nurse Tillman!" called the physician to the head nurse. "Shannon?" he asked again, raising his head this time to look at his trusted friend and professional.

"It's ok Dr. Abel. She's still with us," she continued.

"Pulse is one twenty," returned the nurse. Alison could hear everyone in the room, but their voices were blurry. She was exhausted. Attempting to open her eyes again, she called out to the only other woman's voice in the sterile room.

"Where am I nurse? Shannon?" she continued. Alison remembered the name called by the doctor.

"Alison, I'm here," returned the middle-aged nurse as she walked towards the patient lying squarely on the hospital table. Alison was sweating, but cold and covered in warm blankets. "You're at the Swedish Medical Center in Seattle and your safe now," she continued, calmly stroking the patient's wet hair.

"What just happened, Dr. Abel?" whispered the other specialist in the room.

"I'm not sure Dr. Curtis, but I think we just brought her back from her deathbed. She was without a stable pulse for over two minutes." The badly bruised patient who minutes before was knocking on death's door, was now awake on the recovery table.

The anesthesiologist had turned off the medicine drip a few minutes earlier as the team of doctors were convinced she had not made it. Her massive internal bleeding had stopped. Aside from minor blood seeping from the incision, clamps and pads still inside her, the patient's condition seemed to reverse course almost immediately.

"Sam, did you see what just happened to her blood flow?" referring to the near instant change to the patient. Dr. Rapp and Dr. Curtis stood silently in amazement.

"I've never seen anything like it before," shot back Dr. Abel as he removed his surgical micro-glasses to ensure that he was not hallucinating.

"Ms. Watson. It's nice to have you back again," spoke the head surgeon. "We're going to take care of just a few things and then we'll see you in a little while in the recovery room. Sound ok?" he continued.

"Shannon, let's close her back up and finish with this patient. I've got some interesting reports to write on this case for sure and then, someone important to call."

"Amy, anesthesia again, please," he stated, nodding to the anestiaologist. "Thirty minutes or so should do it. Start at 140-200 μg/kg/min of Propofol please."

"Alison, we're going to put you back to sleep for a bit," stated the physician. "We'll see you in just a little while," he continued as the anesthesiologist injected the milky-white fluid into the intravenous drip. The drug flowed into Alison's veins. Within moments, Ms. Watson was asleep again, but thankfully alive.

Forty minutes later, the surgery was completed. "Dr. Curtis, please close. I've got to make a call," he concluded and walked towards the surgical room exit door. Dr. Sam Abel left the room and pulled his mask down from his face. The operating room doors scissor-kicked back and forth behind him. The remaining medical professionals in the room got back to work. "Suture," called out Dr. Curtis. "Let's go people. We have a young woman who needs our help," he commanded.

* * *

Dream Challenge

Tony woke from his violent dream, coughing heavily as he sat up in bed. It was 4:00 a.m. and still dark. Drenched in sweat and burning up, he pulled the remaining covers off his body. Still breathing heavily, he continued to cough, reaching for a portion of the crumpled cotton sheet to cover his mouth.

"Holy shit," he whispered aloud, trying to regain control of his breathing. After glancing at the clock once more, he reached for the light switch. "I've got to get these things out of my head," he muttered as he rose and walked to the bathroom for some cold water. The lights now on, he stood still, hands on the sink, and stared into the mirror.

Blood trickled over his lower lip and down his chin. Tony raced back into the bedroom and grabbed the sheet that he had just used as a makeshift tissue. It too was covered with blood. As his heart and mind continued to race, he coughed a third time, this time directly into his cupped hands. Blood spattered into his open palms. "Oh my God!" cried Tony as he raced back into the bathroom to spit the remaining blood and saliva into the sink. Globs of crimson dotted the porcelain sink as if a paintball shot had exploded on a white hard surface. Tony turned the cold water handle and clear water rushed out of the faucet. He grabbed a hand towel to wipe his face and then raced to the phone and dialed. Two rings, then a third before he finally heard her voice.

"Melissa," he frantically called out to her.

"Tony?"

"I need your help! I am coughing up lots of blood. I need your help now!" he said, breaking into tears.

"Go right to the emergency room," replied Melissa, trying to stay calm. "I'll meet you there."

"Ok. I am going to walk. There's no way I'll be able to catch a cab at this hour," stated Tony.

"Thank God you're so close to the hospital," replied Melissa. "Tony, baby. I will be there ok? I'm calling an Uber now," continued Melissa.

"Thanks M. I'm leaving now," said Tony before promptly hanging up the phone and heading back to his bedroom to get dressed.

Quickly, he put on some sweat pants, sneakers, and a tee shirt. Before leaving for the hospital, Tony grabbed a towel from the bathroom and brushed his teeth. Blood continued to seep from his mouth. Keeping the towel in his right hand and moving to the center room, he grabbed his wallet off the coffee table and abruptly left the apartment.

As he reached the street, the moist and chilly air confronted him. The only light to guide him was provided by the half-moon in the clear sky along with alternating corner streetlights. Tony turned briskly and walked the sidewalk, occasionally dabbing his mouth to soak up the blood that was still flowing. Turning right onto North Central Street, he headed towards the city's premier hospital – Massachusetts General Hospital. The prestigious institution was only a half mile from his apartment. Half way there, Tony paused and dropped to one knee on the grass writhing in pain. His joints had become increasingly stiff. Sharp pain shot down his legs.

"God, please help me," he called softly, looking up at the stars as he stood and rubbed his legs in a downward motion, alternating from left to right and back again.

"Mother of God, this hurts," he continued. As he neared the hospital, Tony started to feel a level of comfort and hoped that the doctors would help him return to his normal life. Limping now from the pain in his legs, he passed through the automatic doors into the emergency room and walked up to the registration area.

"May I help you?" asked the pretty clerk serving the graveyard shift.

"Yes, please. I need a doctor immediately. I'm coughing up blood and have significant pain in my arms and legs.

"Ok, but we'll need to get some information from you about your insurance company," she returned.

"Lady, I need to see a doctor now!" Reaching into his wallet, Tony retrieved the insurance card and slapped it down on the counter before heading back into the emergency room triage area.

"Wait, stop!" called the woman. Tony had already passed the entrance to the section of the hospital where busy doctors and nurses were tending to other patients. A police officer standing in the lobby moved towards Tony to intervene. "Officer. Wait.

It's ok. He's in pretty bad shape," she continued. "Let's let him go through this time."

"Are you sure miss?" asked one of Boston's finest, one hand on his night stick, the other on the outside of his holster.

"Yes, I'm sure. I will process his paperwork for him and pass it back to the ER staff in a few minutes. He looks like he's in a lot of pain." Tony walked directly up to the nurse's station and asked to see a doctor immediately.

"Nurse, can I please see a doctor?" I'm coughing up blood like a pirate," he said jokingly, but in obvious pain.

"Come with me please," returned the aging nurse. Seeing he was in pain, she grabbed a clipboard, assisted Tony to curtain room 14B, and pulled the screen closed. "Tell me what the problem is," she asked with pencil in hand. Tony proceeded to explain his symptoms to the nurse, leaving out no details and providing a degenerative history of his problems over the past three days. The nurse dutifully documented everything she heard. "A doctor will be right with you. Please stay here Mr. Blackwell," she asked before walking out of the portable examination room. *The hospital was shockingly busy at this hour with customers,* thought Tony. That was Mass General. It was one of the busiest hospitals in Boston.

Minutes later, Doctor Walter Robinson pulled the curtain back and sat down next to Tony.

"Mr. Blackwell, tell me a little more about your problem," politely asked the doctor.

Tony proceeded to tell the young medical professional his symptoms, starting most recently with the fact that he had been spitting spoonfuls of blood.

"May I?" asked the doctor before pulling back his sweat pant leg. To his amazement, the doctor paused and cautiously explored the many bruises on Tony's leg. "Are they sensitive?" touching one of the larger ones.

"Ouch!" replied Tony. "Of course they hurt," he continued. "How long have you been practicing medicine?" he rudely asked. The question and answer session continued for almost ten minutes between patient and physician. Just when he thought the doctor was out of questions to ask, Tony heard the sound of Melissa's voice as she asked to see her boyfriend.

"Melissa, I'm in here," called Tony as he jumped to his feet and pulled the curtain back.

"Tony!" replied Melissa as she rushed to him and hugged him for what seemed like an eternity, a clear sign of her affection. She was concerned and rightfully so. Melissa sat down next to her man on the rolling bed. The doctor continued to ask Tony a series of additional questions and then ordered up blood work for the patient.

"Mr. Blackwell, from what you've explained to me, with your stressful job and all, it wouldn't surprise me if you have an ulcer that has ruptured," stated Dr. Robinson.

"An ulcer?" questioned Melissa. "How in the hell do you explain those bruises on his arms and legs and the stiffness in his joints doctor?" she pressed.

"That, I don't have an answer for yet miss. I'm ordering up a full set of blood work to see if we can get to the bottom of that," he continued as he motioned to the nurse to assist. "For now, I'm going to give you some medicine for your stomach and put you on an intravenous drip to provide you some nutrients. You can stay here and be admitted or stay for a short while we hydrate you and then contact you in the morning as soon as the blood tests are back. Your choice."

"He's not going anywhere," returned Melissa. "And I'd like someone checking in on him every couple of hours to make sure his condition isn't getting worse too," she continued with authority. As the doctor left the examination room, Melissa promptly closed the curtain for privacy.

"Melissa. I had another one of those dreams last night." Pausing before he continued, Tony poured a glass of water from the plastic pitcher next to the bed and gulped it down. "As soon as I woke up, I was spitting up blood," he continued. Melissa sat there for ten minutes as Tony explained the entire dream challenge. He told her all the gory details of the dream, except the part about Alison and the kiss. "What bothers me M is that each time I fail one of these things and wake up, it seems like my health is going downhill fast. I mean, look at me!"

"Listen Tony. I'm starting to believe you about all this dream challenge stuff, I really am," she said touching his arm. "I'm going back to talk to the doctor to see if there is someone else we can talk to about this problem."

"You mean a shrink? If you think I am going to see some psychobabble doctor, you're nuts."

"No, not one of those doctors," she interrupted. "A professional that can help us understand what these dreams mean and how to stop them. I read about a medical specialty in the New York Times about a year ago, where they do a series of tests while patients dream. If you can just get control of your dreams, or not even dream at all, maybe this whole thing will just go away," she said with optimism and a smile on her face, concealing the real fear inside her.

"Ok, ok. See what you can find out. I'm exhausted and going to close my eyes for a little while."

"Aren't you worried about dreaming again?" she asked.

"Not until tonight," he replied, eyes closed. "They only happen at night and never two in a row in the same day. God, listen to me. I'm starting to predict these stupid things," eyes still shut. Melissa covered Tony with a blanket and headed out in search of a doctor that could help.

* * *

Melissa continued to scan over the various Internet articles she'd found after her consultation with Dr. Richardson. The hospital had several experts in psychotic dreams with therapy to help patients overcome a variety of sleep disorders. Tony needed them along with a good internist.

"Polysomnography recording of brain waves, CPAP/BiPAP titration study. Shoot! I'm in way over my head," mumbled Melissa as she scrolled through online research articles and medical jargon describing various sleep disorder conditions. Dr. Robinson had recommended a specialist named Pete Smith. Melissa glanced at her watch. It was 8:45 a.m. and Dr. Smith was supposedly due in the office at 9:00 a.m. She continued patiently waiting outside his office in the left wing of the hospital while reading. *Fifteen more minutes*, she thought. *God, I hope Tony will be all right.*

* * *

Alison lay in the hospital recovery room, feeling better and more chipper than the last few days. The nurses and doctors checked her vitals every sixty minutes and were simply dumbfounded at the speed of her recovery.

"Can you believe that she just came back from the dead like that and now, she's eating and her bruises are healing at a pace that we've never seen before?" chatted one of the nurses at the station down the hall from Alison's room.

"I'm telling you, it's like we had a miracle or something in this hospital," replied another nurse while flipping through the chart of another patient.

"Hi," interrupted a young woman with a bouquet of flowers and a big stuffed cheetah animal. "I'm here to see Alison Watson. Can you tell me what room she's in?"

"Sure sweetie. 3011," replied the nurse. "Just down the hall and to the right," she continued, pointing in the approximate direction of the room. Rachel Whittaker politely knocked on the door and passed through the archway.

"Hey girl. How's my favorite dream nut job?" joked her friend as she approached the bed.

"Hey Rachel. I am so glad you are here. Close the door, will you? I have so much to tell you." The dutiful friend placed the gifts on the bed over Alison's legs and complied with the request. "Come on, hurry up!" Rachel scurried over to an open chair, dragged it to her friend's bed, and sat down next to her. She leaned in as if she was going to hear the story of her life.

"So, I finally beat that son-of-a-bitch last night," stated Alison.

"No way. How did you do it?" Alison proceeded to tell her confidant all about the most recent dream and even about Tony, sparing no detail. What seemed like an hour passed as the two close friends caught up about the dream challenge and life in general. Alison ended up talking more about Tony and the Egyptian vault than her triumph over Mr. Y in the fighter jet.

"So. Could you feel it when you kissed him?" asked Rachel, seemingly on the edge of her seat.

"Yeah, I could," replied Alison with a warm smile on her face before both girls erupted with laughter. "It was so real. Listen. I'm hoping to get out of here in a day or so. Can you do me a favor?"

"Sure. Anything."

"Ok. Don't think I'm crazy or anything, but I've got to know if this dream stuff is really just a bunch of dreams or something else," said Alison.

"What do you mean?"

"I mean, I want you to Google Tony Blackwell and see what you come up with."

"Come on Alison. You have to be kidding. I mean these are just dreams," replied Rachel.

"I am sure they are, but what if this guy really exists?" she shot back. "I mean, really, what if he is real?"

"If he is real, then I am calling the Paddy Wagon!" shot back her friend.

"Just do it, ok? I'm not crazy," whispered Alison.

"Ok." At that exact moment, the hospital attendee came through the door with medicine for Alison.

"Hello sunshine. How is the patient today?" she asked.

"I'm fine and feeling better every hour," replied Alison.

"Great. Keep taking your medicine and you'll be good as new in no time," stated the nurse. "Your breakfast should be here in a few minutes too, so you and your friend should wrap things up," she continued. Alison and Rachel said their goodbyes for the day.

"Now, you get well fast ok? Everybody back at Microsoft is waiting for you to come back to work. They are so tired of covering your accounts," she joked.

"Remember. Google," called out Alison as her friend exited the room. Her friend replied with a simple nod and then headed out of the room to start her day back at the Seattle software giant.

* * *

"Mr. Blackwell. We just got back your blood work," stated Dr. Robinson. His steely expression matched the perfectly combed gray hair on his head. "It does not contain anything out of the ordinary from what I can see."

"Then why am I feeling like hell?" replied Tony.

"I am not sure, but that is why we are going to keep you here for a little while longer. I would like to run some additional tests and see how you progress over the next two days. Can you tell me what you are feeling at this moment?"

"Yes. My back aches like hell and I feel like I have arthritis all over my body. I mean I am *sore*. Really sore all over."

"Any more blood?"

"No. Just this morning. It happened right after I woke up from a dream," replied Tony. "I also have a raging headache right now. Can you explain why I am bruised all over my body?"

"No, I cannot, but I am going to call another colleague to take a look at you and see what he thinks."

"What kind of doctor, a shrink?" asked Tony. "Because I don't need a shrink!" he said, elevating his voice.

"Calm down Tony," said Melissa, taking Tony's hand.

"No Mr. Blackwell. An infectious disease expert," replied Dr. Robinson.

"What on earth for?" asked Melissa.

"So that we can get to the bottom of this Miss," replied the experienced physician. "Unfortunately, Tony's symptoms and the rate at which he's developed them, are above my expertise," replied the doctor. "In the meantime, we have got a good dream expert working with you to see if we can isolate what is happening when you sleep and if there is a connection to your physical state," concluded Dr. Robinson. "For now, just keep taking the medicine for your stomach to see if we can quell the internal bleeding. Also, I've prescribed some pain medication." Just then, Doctor Smith walked into the room.

"Hi Tony. I am Doctor Peter Smith. We are going to hook up some electrodes now and set the machines to record everything while you sleep," stated the specialist physician. "The EEG measures and records four forms of brain wave activities – alpha, beta, delta, and theta waves. The electromyogram (EMG) will record muscle activity, such as teeth grinding, facial twitches, and any leg or arm movements. This will help me determine your stage of sleep and the readings for each stage. I am especially interested in your REM, or rapid eye movement. The equipment will tell me how long it takes to get you to REM and what your vitals are like during that important stage of sleep," continued the doctor.

"What happens if I get disconnected from all this crap if I move around too much?" asked Tony. Melissa increased her grip on Tony's hand as the conversation continued.

"Don't worry. Most people don't really move around that much when they dream," replied the physician. "I am also going to record the entire evening via a night-vision video camera system. We will get to the bottom of this. I promise you," he continued.

"I will leave the two of you alone for a few minutes, and then unfortunately, I am going to have to ask this pretty little lady to go home."

"Thanks doctor," replied Tony.

"You will be fine Tony. I like this guy," said Melissa in a comforting tone. "Are you getting tired or will they need to give you something to help you fall asleep?"

"No on both. I have to be honest M. I kind of want to fall asleep and beat this son-of-a-bitch at his challenges."

"Then you are going to have to calm down so that you can go to sleep."

"Ok, ok," replied Tony. "Listen. You should head home. I will be fine."

"I love you Tony."

"Love you too M," smiled Tony. Melissa let go of his hand and walked out of the room, giving Tony the needed space to get comfortable and sleep. Tony turned on the television, scanning stations until he found an international soccer game. "That should do it," he said jokingly. "This will put me out." After Dr. Smith's resident assistant connected the sensors and turned on the video camera along with the EEG machine, the television and the power light from the video recording system provided some additional light in the room.

"You are all set," stated the resident as she headed for the door. "Sweet dreams," she concluded, closing the door so that Tony could have some privacy. Forty-five minutes later, Tony's eyelids succumbed to the weight of gravity and gently closed shut.

12 – SHOOT FOR THE MOON

Tara Holloway, Tony Blackwell, and a new young male contestant stood on fine red, sand-like dirt, each fully encased in black space suits equipped with breathing apparatus. Tony gazed around as he raised his arms to determine how confined the metal space suit would affect his movement. As he looked around, all he could see was the combination of a reddish hue intersecting with large lava rock formations that seemed to compliment the eerie atmosphere. No other humans, buildings, or roads, were visible.

"What the hell are we doing here?" asked Tony, still taking in his surroundings. "What the," he stated, pausing as he pointed upwards to the sky at a forty-five degree angle to the ground. "Is that Earth?" he continued.

"Why, yes it is," returned the host of the evening's festivities. Mr. Y was hovering near the group, but in front of a cavernous entrance to a hole in the ground that resembled the start of a tunnel cut that directly into the rocky landscape.

"How is this even possible?" asked Tony.

"You're in my world, Mr. Blackwell. Anything is possible," replied the host, still outfitted in his white robe and not showing his lower extremities. He was not wearing a space suit. Tony wondered if the atmosphere had enough oxygen to sustain human life, but did not want to risk taking off his helmet and suffocating himself on the moon-like planet.

"Where is Alison Watson!" demanded Tony.

"Mr. Blackwell. Do you miss her?" replied Mr. Y.

"What have you done with her?" pressed Tony.

"Well, if you must know. She's alive and well, and back living her life. You see Mr. Blackwell. She completed one of her seven dream challenges. That means she lives."

"Lives? What the hell are you talking about?" questioned Tony.

"Who is Alison Watson?" asked the new contestant with a quizzical expression on his face.

"I demand that you bring her back. I need to see her again," interrupted Tony.

"Well, that is a little harder than you might think," replied Mr. Y. "But doable. I do caution you though Mr. Blackwell, as there may be consequences beyond your control," he continued.

"What consequences?" shot back Tony.

"As part of your seven night dream challenge, a contestant may bring back a prior contender who passed one of the challenges, but only once," he continued. "But, if you do so, I reset the clock on that contestant's challenge. Thus, she will start her clock at one again and if she does not complete one of her seven challenges, she will die in real life," explained the host with arms extended high into the air.

"Die?" muttered Tony.

"What do you mean die?" questioned the new candidate. "Does that mean that we also die if we do not complete one of these stupid things? And I don't even know what these things are," stated the new contestant with frustration clearly in his voice.

"Yes, Mr. Newel. You will die," returned the host, staring into Tony's eyes as he answered Mike Newel's question. "Oh yes, there is one more rule. You may not reveal these rules to any candidates who are brought back into the game," continued Mr. Y. "If you do so and do not succeed at your challenge, you will also die, regardless of what number challenge you are on."

"So if I elect to bring her back, I cannot tell her that she has seven tries to stay alive again?" asked Tony.

"That is correct, Mr. Blackwell. So what is it going to be? Are you really willing to take Ms. Watson's fate into your own hands?" Tony paused for a long while before answering. He looked around at the environment again, taking in the near-abandoned moon-like atmosphere.

"Bring her back," demanded Tony. "I have got to see her again."

"As you wish, Mr. Blackwell. As you wish," answered Mr. Y. The host snapped his fingers in conjunction with the last word he spoke. Instantly, Alison stood in place of Mike Newel, who was now gone from the game. Looking a bit confused, she glanced around before recognizing both Tony and Mr. Y.

"What the hell am I doing back here?" demanded Alison. "I beat you!" she yelled, now staring directly at the hovering host as she began to cry. As Tony attempted to move towards Alison, the constriction of the space suit combined with zero gravity, greatly slowed his forward progress.

"Alison, I am so sorry. Do not be angry. I had to bring you back," stated Tony, now directly in front of her. Tony and Alison stared at one another through their space helmets.

"What did you do? I do not understand Tony. What were you thinking?" she pressed. Tony proceeded to tell Alison that he had fallen for her and had to see her again. He did not, however, reveal the rules of engagement for the challenges as Mr. Y had cautioned him.

"I am sorry Alison. I just had to see you again and this was the only way I could do it."

"What do you say we both beat this son-of-a-bitch and get out of here once and for all?" whispered Alison, helmets pressed together. Tony nodded.

"Ok all. Time to get back to the festivities," called Mr. Y. "Tonight I have a special treat for you. Each of you will have four minutes to find the flag that best represents your heritage inside the cave entrance, before you return and pass *this* white line before me. Mr. Y promptly jabbed a checkered flag into the boxed area just next to the finish line." Each contestant contemplated their quest, but did not speak. "The fun part of this challenge is that you will all be competing together at the same time. If there is a conflict for one of the flags, one or more of you will lose, as there is only one flag per country.

"Where are the flags? Inside that cave?" asked Tara, pointing to the entrance.

"Yes, Ms. Holloway. Everything you need is inside. Ok everybody, we start in one minute. Please move towards the line and take your place side by side."

"Why four minutes? We're usually given much less time," asked Alison.

"Zero-gravity warrants that I give you more time for less gravity Ms. Watson," replied Mr. Y.

The three cosmonauts-like contestants complied with the host's request and slowly moved towards the line. As they walked, each tested their suits flexibility and restrictions in their own way. Tony hopped with his feet together like a basketball player getting ready to dunk, demonstrating to the others that the gravity was very thin.

"Is everyone ready? Three, two, one, go!" called Mr. Y as he started the stopwatch. Tony, Alison, and Tara raced to enter the cave at the same time, each running a bit on the clumsy side. Within moments, Alison and Tony arrived together at the cave's entrance, leading Tara by five seconds. Three tunnels came into view just past the crest of the hill leading downward into the cave.

"Which one?" called out Alison.

"I have a good feeling about the right one," replied Tony. The pair moved together side by side, descending into the cave's darkness. Torches burned brightly and lined the right side of the cave. Knowing that it took oxygen to maintain fire, Tony paused briefly before opening his helmet. Once the seal was broken, air flushed into his lungs.

"What are you doing?" called Alison, now stopped after noticing that Tony had not kept pace with her.

"There is oxygen on this red planet Alison." After three or four deep breaths with his helmet partially opened, Tony removed the constraining metal shell and dropped it to the ground. The impact caused a slow release of red sand into the air around the steel shell.

"How much time do we have left?" Alison briefly looked at her watch.

"I'm not sure. I did not look at my watch when we started," she replied. Tony started to run again after briefly contemplating taking off his entire suit to allow him to move freer and faster. "Let's go!" pushed Alison. The pair continued their race through the tunnel.

Tara Holloway could no longer see Tony and Alison. She chose the left tunnel and was moving through it quite rapidly. As she descended into the mountain, the light disappeared, causing her to stop when it was completely black. Tara reached up to turn on a light attached to the top of her helmet. She had noticed that the two other contestants had a light on their helmet and assumed that she had one as well. A small rotation to the right resulted in a clear stream of white light. A stream of water ran along the full length of the ceiling, continuing into the remainder of the tunnel. *The ceiling*, thought Tara. *How could that be?* The fluid flowed quickly, but did not drop to the ground, defying gravity. Tara reached up to touch the water, believing it was some kind of hallucination. It was not.

The touch from her suit caused the clear liquid to drop to the ground. The remaining water continued to flow downhill, but upside down. Tara quickly became aware of the distraction and restarted her run through the tunnel.

Colorful crystals lined the cave on either side of the stream. Red, green, and white objects of different sizes and shapes protruded from the jagged walls, some with sharp edges as the light from her helmet beamed into the cave. Towards the end of the tunnel, bones of large mammal-like skulls rested on the ground. Some of them were quite large, with large irregular shaped heads, many with mouths wide open.

Patterns on the wall in white chalk resemble those of other non-human forms, seeming to tell a story about life in the cave or on the planet. As she continued to run, she could see a light at the end of her path. As she passed through the end of the tunnel, she was standing inside a large room with smooth steel walls that ran almost twenty feet tall. She saw Tony and Alison standing on the other side of the room near a rack of objects hanging from the wall.

"Hey you guys!" called out Tara.

"Over here," returned Tony, motioning for her to come to their side of the room. The ceiling was black and interlaced with long and sharp stalactites. Four beams of bright lights shined upwards revealing a hundred or so country flags, all of which hung upside down with their support poles anchored in between the natural projection of colorful elements. The lights, recessed into the seam of the floor and steel walls, were so powerful that the group could not look directly at them.

"Check these out," stated Tony as he removed a crossbow from the rack firmly mounted on the shiny metal wall closest to him. A series of other objects hung on a rack side by side, appearing to be some kind of ancient torture equipment. Whips, spears, spiked balls with chains, and long swords adorned the wall.

"Come on, grab one and try to get the right flag down," called out Alison as she reached for the spear. Tara and Alison removed their helmets and took a deep breath as Tony had done some time back. As she pulled the long metal spear from the wall, she noticed that it still had dried blood on one side that ran half the length of the shaft.

"Gross!" shouted Alison, dropping the object to the floor. Tony bent down to retrieve it, stunned by the dried red blood.

"Just use it to get the American flag Alison. We have got to get it down and get the hell out of here!" continued Tony. Tara moved closer to the wall and retrieved one of the metal ball and chains. They were surprisingly light, likely assisted by the lack of gravity. After moving towards the center of the room, Tara found the United Kingdom flag two-thirds the way towards the left side. Holding onto one end of the linked chain, she swung the weapon, generating a whirring and clanking sound, as the outer ball gained speed while rotating in a circle.

"Ah!" called out Tara as she released the rotating ball-like helicopter blade towards the ceiling. The balls slammed into a group of flags right near the British Union Jack flag. Several other flags fell to the floor.

"Get out of the way!" called Tony as the flags fell towards the ground. They came down in a coordinated spear attack. Tara moved out of the way just in time for the flags to hit the ground. Some of them pierced the sandy floor and remained vertical.

"Thanks Tony," sighed Tara. Tony, still focused, carefully pulled three wooden arrows with deadly sharp points from the wall rack and inserted the first into the drawn crossbow. Aiming at the base of the American flag, he pulled the trigger and fired. The arrow swooshed through the air and pierced into the ceiling as it deflected slightly off a nearby stalactite.

"Shit," responded Tony. As he loaded another arrow into the bay of the crossbow, Alison launched a spear at the same target. The spear careened off the ceiling and fell to the ground. Seconds later, Tara hurled the linked swirling steel balls into the air again, yelling as she put all of her muscles into the effort. The balls turned and rotated in unison as they approached the target. As it neared the ceiling, the whirling weapon wrapped around the UK flag pole and snapped it in half. The remaining part of the pole locked into the ceiling, as the flag and lower portion fell to the floor.

She instinctively stepped aside as the flag's spear-like cap, adorned with an eagle, landed at an eighty-degree angle to the ground. The flagstick vacillated from side to side for a few moments before it stabilized and stopped moving. Tara grabbed the remainder of the broken shaft of the UK flag and started to run back to the planet surface.

Instantly, the ground and the cave began to shake. Some of the stalactites from the ceiling separated from their inverted base and rained down on the cosmonauts.

"Alison, look out!" called Tony as he dropped the loaded crossbow and ran towards his virtual girlfriend. Upon hitting the ground, the crossbow accidentally fired its payload. The arrow swooshed a few feet above Alison's head, then careened off the steel-like wall before it fell back to the ground.

"Tony?" questioned Alison as she tried to protect her head from the falling rocks. "What is happening?" she continued, now down on one knee.

"I don't know, but it looks like this place is coming down. We have to try again." Tony bent down and picked up the spear and readied a throw. As he focused on the target above, the ground continued to rumble as stalactites rained down on the two of them.

"Now!" yelled Alison. Tony launched the spear into the light air. The spear raced upwards. As the two stared upwards in fear, the spear expertly struck the intersection of the ceiling and the base of the American flag. Instantly, the flag and pole began to fall.

"Yeah," called out Tony as he pushed Alison out of the way of the falling object. It landed just a few feet away from where Alison stood. "Let's go!" he said as he reached down for the prize and started to run back into the tunnel. Alison happily pursued him as the ground continued to rumble under their feet.

Tara picked the rightmost tunnel and ran back to the planet's surface. As she entered the tunnel and turned the corner, an automated escalator came into view. She stopped and paused for a moment, then took the runway-like metal stairs with blinking lights towards the surface. Tara turned around, only to see that the tunnel was gone and replaced with a pile of rocks. Short on time, she turned back and raced up the stairs. Knowing that the space suit would prevent her from running quickly up the narrow walkway, she instinctively put one foot in front of the other and progressed at a speed that wouldn't make her fall.

"Come on," she muttered. Flashes of light danced along the wall of rock that surrounded the escalator's rising tunnel shell. Some patterns circled her exact location on the steps, while other flashes of bright yellow and orange lights raced along the walls in the opposite direction, giving her the feeling that she was moving at a tremendous pace. She just stared at the light show in amazement and pondered the Holloway English family crest and history. Within moments, Tara could see light at the end of the escalator's exit, growing brighter with every second she rode the lift.

"Thank God," she mused, still firmly grasping her prized flag. Alison and Tony selected the leftmost tunnel entrance and continued to run as fast as they could.

"Tony, wait. Stop!" called Alison, still trailing him. Tony complied and turned around.

"What is it Alison? We have to keep going," he continued impatiently.

"You keep the flag," she returned.

"What do you mean?"

"Only one of us can cross the line with the flag and I am telling you that it is going to be you!" she demanded.

"We'll do it together and hold the flag at the same time," returned Tony.

"No! We will both be disqualified. You take it. I have beaten this guy before and can do it again."

"Alison. Everything will be,"

"Stop it Tony, just go!" she interrupted as she pushed him forward to start running. "Trust me."

Tony against his best judgment began to run again and harder this time, seemingly with more focus. As the pair ran, the ground continued to rumble and cracks began to show in the large tunnel's inner shell. "Faster!" pushed Alison. Within moments, the pair could see the cave's entrance and light from the surface. The rumbling seemed to intensify in both frequency and damage, causing rocks to fall from the ceiling as the sides of the tunnel started to collapse.

"Stay with me Alison!" shouted Tony as his mind continued to race for a solution that would allow both he and Alison to win the challenge together. "Shit!" he muttered as a softball sized rock careened off his shoulder, almost hitting his exposed head. "We are almost there," he continued, looking back to make sure she was right behind him. Alison ran right behind him, her arms extended above her head in a crossed pattern to protect her exposed body.

As the pair passed out of the tunnel and started the mild climb to the crest of the hill, they could see Tara running for the finish line. She was a good fifteen seconds ahead of them. The pair raced up the hill, exhaustion setting in on both of them. Their pace slowed as they ran past the top of the hill.

"Thank God," exclaimed Alison as they ran towards the finish line.

"Grab the flag with me Alison!" called out Tony as the pair ran as hard as they could, gravity still preventing them from a swift pace. Alison grabbed onto the exposed flagpole with her left hand, causing Tony to smile briefly. As Tony and Alison closed in on the finish line, they could see Tara firmly jam her flagpole into the boxed area just passed the white line. Mr. Y closely monitored her time via his trusty watch. Tara immediately collapsed once the flag stood firmly in the reddish dirt, rolled over to her back, and gazed at the stars above the eerie planet she inhabited.

"Well done Ms. Holloway. You passed in three minutes, fifty five seconds," continued Mr. Y as he snapped his fingers. Tara began to float upwards and levitate, still in a horizontal position to the ground. Mr. Y's hand was now extended towards her, seeming to control the pace and height of her levitated body. As Tony and Alison raced across the finish line and towards the box, Mr. Y focused his attention on the stopwatch, still keeping Tara levitated. As Tony crossed into the boxed area, Alison took her hand off the flagpole.

"What are you doing?" called Tony, pausing for a brief moment.

"Jam the flag into the ground!" demanded Alison. Confused, Tony complied. Dropping to his knees, he plunged the broken wooden base into the ground and released his grip on the United States flag.

"You fail Mr. Blackwell," smiled Mr. Y. "Four minutes and ten seconds."

"Shit!" called out Tony in anger as he rose to his feet in defiance of the result.

"You too, Ms. Watson," continued Mr. Y, now holding up his free hand towards Tony to prevent him from attacking the host. The stopwatch rope dangled from Mr. Y's wrist and swung side to side as he kept Tony in place. Mr. Y raised his other hand upwards, causing Tara to rise at an increasing pace. Within seconds, she was no longer visible to Tony.

"Where did she go?" demanded Tony.

"She won Mr. Blackwell," returned Mr. Y. "You two did not," he continued. *Snap!*

13 – BLOOD FROM A STONE

Alison woke up from her dream in a sweat on Sunday morning. Her heart pumped faster than normal. The covers were in shambles on her bed.

Dammit, she said to herself. The sun rose above the North Cascades mountain range as she began her new day. Looking at her watch, Alison sprang off the bed, headed to the den in her tiny little apartment, and turned on the television. "Come on," she commanded as she waited for the local Seattle news station to provide highlights. Not satisfied with the response time, she turned and grabbed her smart phone off the table.

"Thank God it's Sunday," she exhaled, knowing that she could relax before heading back to work tomorrow. It was 7:15 a.m. and Alison dialed the all too familiar phone number. Three rings. "Rachel, it's me. I had another one of those dreams again last night! I have to see you. Why is this happening again?" she continued. The pair talked more about the dream that took place on a distant planet and agreed to meet for lunch at a local restaurant. "Please come by yourself too. I don't want to discuss this with anyone else."

* * *

Susan Nelson stood next to the table above her patient of only three days. He had come into the Sydney-based hospital complaining of all-around pain and bruised extremities. Blood tests revealed nothing out of the ordinary. Bruising and swelling continued to get worse and eventually the patient bled to death days later. Blood seeped from his eyes at the final hour. The heart monitor tone was constant.

"Please turn that thing off," snapped Dr. Nelson. "Time of death is 8:01 a.m." After giving instructions to the other physicians, she retreated to her office to review the information she had recorded about the strange case. As she flipped through the pages, she scanned for anything abnormal. Twenty-seven year old male. No history of kidney or liver disease. Blood tests all seemed normal. Complaints of internal bleeding four days ago, massive bruising, muscle aches, but a normal pulse and blood pressure. "I don't get it," she commented to herself.

Frustrated and tired, Susan dialed her assistant via a one-touch button on her IP-enabled phone. "Missy, my report is complete. Please send my report to Richard Lewis at the CDC. He needs to know about this case." The conversation was short. After she hung up the phone, Dr. Nelson removed her glasses and rubbed her eyes, before she turned on her computer. Her colorful surgery scrub hat still adorned her head. She had been up half the night trying to prevent the most recent catastrophe. *I must be missing something.*

* * *

At 9:00 a.m., Tony Blackwell rested in his hospital bed after a difficult night of restless sleep. Dr. Peter Smith sat in his office and reviewed the data captured from the evening's session. The alpha and beta numbers, seemed in line, but the delta and theta numbers were off the charts. *How could that be?* The physician pushed the play button on the DVD to review Tony's REM. While Tony was in REM, the delta and theta numbers went crazy. Dr. Smith leaned in to see the other information from the film. What he witnessed over the next ten minutes was disturbing. Tony initially seemed comfortable as he entered REM. Dr. Smith expected some minor muscle and eye movement just prior to his patient achieving dream state. Then it happened.

Tony's body jerked violently on the bed. His head randomly snapped from side to side with no apparent series of coordinated timing. Tony's arms and legs also moved more than normal and at times, he attempted to speak. Random teeth chattered. As Dr. Smith rewound the video, he focused his attention on the audio.

After playing the video three times, he could not make out any of the words, but it seemed that his patient never experience a state of bliss during the time he dreamt. Although Tony's eyes were closed, he was more animated while in a state of sedation. The video appeared more like a patient experiencing a mild epileptic. Baffled by what he had just witnessed, Dr. Smith cross-checked the time of the violent movements with the information recorded by the EEG. There it was. The delta and theta numbers spiked at exactly the same time Tony appeared to be having an unconscious seizure.

* * *

By the time Dr. Smith arrived at Tony's room, Melissa Stewart was there.

"He's awake now doctor. How did the tests go last night?" asked Melissa.

Nodding at Melissa and ignoring her question, Dr. Smith checked on his patient. "How are you feeling today Tony?"

"Sore," he replied, clearly exhausted. "When I woke up, I had some blood coming out of my nose. I went to the bathroom and I," Tony paused. "Melissa, can you excuse us for a moment?" asked Tony politely. "I need to talk to my doctor alone," he continued. Melissa simply nodded, stood up, and walked out of the room. "I'm sorry Dr.

Smith. I just don't want her to worry too much about this."

"I fully understand, Mr. Blackwell. What were you going to tell me?"

"My aches and bruises seem to be getting worse. I had a hard time standing when I went to the bathroom. There was also blood in my urine," he confided.

"Tony, I am going to be honest with you. I don't yet know what is causing your symptoms, but it is serious. These are not normal test results of a healthy young man. I looked at your video along with the data I gathered last night. You are jumping around like a jackrabbit when you are in the middle of rapid eye movement, or REM. Two of the EEG numbers are off the charts. I am going to recommend some medicine to help you relax when you sleep and see if we can get to the bottom of this."

"What type of medicine?"

"A mild-level dose of anti-anxiety, along with a heavy muscle relaxer to see if we can get those aches and pains under control. In addition, I'll do a scope of your stomach tomorrow to see if there are any ulcers causing your bleeding."

"You've got to be kidding me. Ulcers?" questioned Tony. "I'm not an old man doctor."

"I know, but you seem to be under a lot of stress. Melissa and I talked about what is going on at work. Trust me. The tests are designed to help figure out what is going on. In the meantime, the nurse will come in shortly with your medication. Please take it, but no food for the rest of the day. I need twenty-four hours to clear you out before going in for a look. I am going to do the scope first thing in the morning if that's ok with you. Then, I'll re-run the video and look at the results. Ok?" Tony nodded.

"Yep."

"Just one more thing. Is there any history of seizures with you or any members of your immediate family?"

"No. Why on Earth would you ask that?"

"Because it appears you had a seizure last night. Do not worry Mr. Blackwell. I'll get to the bottom of this," he concluded with a confident look on his face.

"Please don't tell Melissa about this. I do not want her to worry. I am going to ask her to go home tonight. Please back me up, will you?"

"Sure thing." Confident he was not. After Dr. Smith walked out of Tony's room, he paused and leaned up against the wall. As he flipped through Tony's chart, he looked for data that would explain the strange symptoms.

Twenty minutes later, after getting a cup of coffee, Melissa came back into the room. At the door, she knocked.

"Come on in M. You do not have to knock."

"I wasn't sure since you asked me to leave," she responded with a sheepish look on her face. "By the way, did you dream again last night?"

"Yes. It was pretty wild and weird. I was on this crazy planet wearing a space suit, looking for an American flag inside an underground rock-like cave."

"What?"

"Yeah, pretty creepy huh?"

"Were there three contestants again?" she asked patiently, trying not to pry, but dying to know.

"Yes. Just the three of us. Me, a woman named Tara, and another woman, but I don't know her name," fabricated Tony.

"What happened?" Tony proceeded to tell Melissa most of the details surrounding the dream, but left out any damaging information about Alison. Five minutes later and showing signs of being tired, he paused.

"Listen. Everything is going to be just fine. I just needed some time to chat man to man with the doctor, ok?" Melissa simply nodded, but did not really understand. She loved Tony so much. "I'd like you to go home and get some rest tonight. Go to work too," he said smiling. "I need a good night's rest tonight. I promise you that if something comes up, I will call your cell."

"You promise?"

"Yes, I promise." The act had worked. She perked up a bit and put on a strong, happy face as she drew near him. Melissa gave Tony a simple peck on the cheek, then walked out of the room. Just before she exited, Melissa held up her cell phone as a reminder. "I get it Melissa. Go. Relax and go back to work. I will be just fine tomorrow with the new medicine that this doctor gave me. I love you."

* * *

"Dr. Lewis. I would like to show you something," stated the young analyst recently recruited from the University of Pennsylvania's medical school. He flipped to page twenty-three of the report. "I think I'm on to something. I have compiled a database of similar unsolved deaths over the last three months with similar symptoms across the globe."

"Does the World Health Organization have this data too?"

"Yes, but not my hypothesis."

"Hypothesis for the cause of symptoms?"

"No, but I think I can predict the certainty of death to within a day or so from the onset of symptoms," replied the young physician and researcher.

"What do you have, Charlie? You now have my full attention for exactly three minutes," responded the elite infectious disease expert.

"Ok. Over the last three months, hospitals from twenty-one countries, most G20, have reported deaths with Ebola-like symptoms within six to seven days of the onset of symptoms."

"Obviously, this is not Ebola or Dengue Fever. I'm listening," continued Dr. Lewis.

"Yes, sir. Patients initially complain of muscle tenderness, and bruising in the first forty-eight hours. The fascinating part of these cases is that all seventy-three patients go on to die from fever and internal bleeding. No survivors!"

"Why hasn't this come to my desk before now?" asked Dr. Lewis angrily.

"Because we don't know the cause and don't think it's an epidemic. All of the doctors that have run tests against the blood-related bio-toxins and non-curable diseases have come up empty."

"Empty? How is that possible?"

"I don't know, but I think that from the data I've gathered on the seventy-three patients, they start to bleed internally on day five and die a couple of days later," he confidently reported, while he touched his glasses for an extra academic flair.

"When was the last reported case?"

"We had another death in Australia last night, with a new case being reported this morning in Boston."

"Where?"

"Mass General by Dr. Peter Smith." The seasoned doctor turned and abruptly walked the other way, forgetting to thank his younger and less experienced colleague for the information he provided.

"Alice!" Get me on a flight to Boston. Today!" he yelled as he walked through the highly populated office filled with world-class physicians, researchers, and statisticians.

14 – UNCHARTED WATERS

Alison, Tony, and a new male contestant sat on a boat just off the shoreline of a tropical island. Lush green and blue water slowly splashed up against the side of the mid-sized fiberglass boat, suitable for six people. Fishing rods stood at attention, almost saluting the blue sky with speckled clouds. Mr. Wilson gazed around, looked at his surroundings, then at the others in the boat. The engine was turned off. The only sound emanated from seagulls above, combined with the sea's subtle side-to-side splashing dance.

"What am I doing here?" asked the new contestant, after a brief pause.

"What is your name?" asked Tony, now a veteran of the challenges. "I am Tony and that's Alison," he continued, pointing to the beautiful woman sporting a low-rise bikini, panty straps tied in a bow as they clung to her shapely hips.

"Casey. Casey Wilson," he calmly replied, turning briefly away from Tony to look at the water, then towards the island.

"Tony, why are we all wearing bathing suits?" asked Alison.

"I don't know, but I can guess," he replied.

"How do you know each other's name?" interjected Casey.

"Dude, I wish I could tell you, but it is for your own good that I don't," replied Tony, remembering the strict rules that Mr. Y had discussed with him. Death after seven failed challenges. *I bet I'm the only one here that knows the rules,* thought Tony. "That is what I get for bringing her back," he muttered.

"What do you get?" asked Alison, briefly hearing his comment as she walked towards him. Alison's balance was influenced by the sway of the boat.

"Nothing. Just nice to see you again," he replied. "By the way. You look great in that bikini," continued Tony. The blue and white horizontal striped suit wrapped around her lean body and exposed her abundant cleavage, leaving nothing to the imagination. Alison promptly sat down next to Tony Blackwell, her leg slightly touched his.

"This bikini top seems a little small for me," joked Alison, as she pulled up on the strings to stretch the top over the exposed portion of her breasts. The tight fitting attire politely complimented her blond hair and blue eyes. Casey looked her up and down, and drank her inside his mind. Tony caught the look and did not like it one bit. He shot back a look of caution to the new competitor. She was *his*.

"Welcome everyone. I am Mr. Y," beamed the host from the captain's chair that had been vacant just moments before. Mr. Y spun around and directly faced the contestants from above.

"Who the hell are you?" asked Casey, outfitted with a set of colorful Jams, with matching orange flip-flops. Casey was not shy. His muscles bulged and showcased a zigzag barbed tattoo on his left arm. His confrontational and cocky personality didn't bother Mr. Y. He didn't even look at his questioner, demonstrating his authority.

"Hey, Charlton Hesston! I said, *who the hell are you?*" questioned Casey again, now standing up, flexing his muscles as if he were looking for a fight.

"Ah yes, Mr. Wilson. I have been expecting you and your *bad attitude*. Please take a seat and I will explain."

Casey attempted to walk towards the ladder leading up to the captain's chair to let this holy-rolling monk know who was in charge on the boat – him. Mr. Y just smiled and raised his hand towards the aggressor and lifted him into the air like a fish out of water.

Casey tried to talk, but instead, just flailed aimlessly in the air. Once he had given up the fight, Mr. Y let his lifeless body hover above the deck for a moment. "That is better," stated the host as he dropped Mr. Wilson on the deck. Alison's fingers crabbed their way across Tony's bare leg and grabbed his left hand. He stared straight ahead at Mr. Y, but acknowledged her with a brush of his thumb over her hand.

"Right, back to tonight's challenge," resumed Mr. Y. "Tonight, you will each have an opportunity to demonstrate your aquatic skills. Beyond this wild rock-of-a-island, is a larger one, that sits directly behind us," he stated, arm outstretched and pointing at the lava-like rocky formation off the boat's stern. Mr. Y began his floating hover down from the upper level.

"How does he do that without any feet?" blurted out Casey, as he stared at the void between the bottom of Mr. Y's robe and the stairs. No one else replied.

"You will have two minutes to swim to shore on the other side and cross the white line on the beach," he continued, arms raised up into the air, with a mirage of the beach and the finish line visible in the sky. *Snap!* The image disappeared. Casey laughed at the proposition.

"Ha, ha! What? What if I just sit my ass on this boat old man and take in the scenery?" asked Casey, arms crossed over his stomach. "She looks pretty hot," said Casey, as he pointed to Alison. "Maybe I will just sit and look at her all day," he continued. "Do you have any beer?"

"You will fail Mr. Wilson," politely replied the host.

"Fail what?"

"I'll go first," volunteered Alison.

"No, Alison. Let Casey go first. We may learn something," replied Tony.

"Go first, go last, shit! I am going now," shot back Casey. "Piece of cake," he continued as he stepped on top of the boat's side railing.

"Before you start young man, you need to know that there are two paths you can take. You can swim around the mini-island if you think you're fast enough, or simply dive underneath it," cautioned the host. "It is about twenty yards under water, end to end, or forty yards extra to go around the side," continued Mr. Y.

"I am plenty fast old man. You ready?" provoked Casey as he kicked off his flip-flops, pulled off his shirt, and got into a ready position.

"Yes. Three, two, one, go!" shouted Mr. Y, as he started his trusty stopwatch. He laughed after concluding the countdown. Casey dove into the water and made a big splash. He immediately started to swim towards the left side of the rock, opting not to dive underneath. Casey Wilson's fast, but inefficient arm strokes, combined with his physical body structure, seemed to work against him. Not all the muscles in the world could help him glide over the water like a lean Olympic swimmer. Alison and Tony stood up to watch the action. Within a minute, Casey disappeared from sight as he rounded the small island. All were silent on the boat as they waited until Tony started to talk.

"Alison, come with me," he said, grabbing her hand and walking to the square opening that led to the lower section of the boat. Mr. Y did not say anything and continued to focus his eyes on the stopwatch.

"How will Mr. Y know if he makes it?" asked Alison, as the pair descended the stairs for some privacy.

"He will know. That freak knows everything," replied Tony. Once downstairs, Tony positioned himself directly in front of Alison and held both of her hands. *She was beautiful and surprisingly not nervous*, he thought.

"Alison. It's my fault you are back in these weird challenges. I can't tell you any more than that," he continued. "I feel badly, but I had to see you again. Please accept my apology," he begged.

"I do," she replied as a small smile arose on her face. Tony leaned in and kissed her, not letting go of her hands. To his surprise, she kissed him back, first with just her lips, then with a soft tongue. When the kiss ended, the pair just stared into each other's eyes.

"Listen, don't worry about me. We can both beat Mr. Y," stated Alison. "We need to be smart about it though. No more sharing flags or anything else," she continued. "Just focus on your challenge and trust that you can do it. When we both beat this guy, we'll find each other," she stated. "I live in Seattle, Washington," she whispered softly.

"Ms. Watson! You are up," called Mr. Y from the deck above.

"Let's go," she said softly, this time leading Tony up the stairs by the hand. He had the pleasure of following her, his eyes locked onto the bottom of her blue and white bikini. He did not know which to focus on more, the snugly fit suit shaped around her derriere, or to imagine what she'd look like without the suit altogether. *Wow. This girl is hot as hell.*

"What happened with Casey?" asked Tony, his hand still attached to Alison's.

"He did not make it in time," stated Mr. Y. "He got nipped by a shark and it slowed him down a bit," continued the host. "Be careful. Blood is in the water now."

"Where did he go?" asked Alison.

"Away, Ms. Watson. He will be back though. Will you?" questioned Mr. Y. Alison knew what she had to do. Beat the challenge and hopefully these dreams would just go away permanently. Alison turned to Tony.

"Remember what I said. Focus."

"Good luck," replied Tony, then he kissed her cheek.

"Are you ready Ms. Watson?" Alison double knotted her bathing suit and climbed up onto the boat's railing. "Three, two, one, go!" called out Mr. Y. Alison dove off the side of the boat and entered the water like an experienced swimmer leaping off the blocks. She entered the water perfectly in a slight pike that caused her to go underneath the water for a moment. Once parallel with the water, she swam a near perfect freestyle stroke, occasionally taking breaths to the side.

"Go Alison!" called Tony from the boat. As she neared the rocks ahead, she stopped to take a deep breath, then plunged below to try and cut the distance to the other side. Tony gazed intensely at the rock. Moments later, Alison re-appeared on the same side of the rock mass she had started from. *Something was wrong*, thought Tony. Then, seemingly with new purpose, Alison dove under water again, feet together, as they followed her below the surface. Tony began to count aloud.

"One, two, three, four, five," and continued until he reached twenty. Still no sign of Alison. Had she made it to the other side? Holding her breath as long as she could, Alison breast stroked her way under the rock and between the sandy ocean floor. She passed through a narrow passageway that was just wide enough for a swimmer or shark to pass. The light shimmered from the surface above, and provided her with a clear path forward.

Tropical fish danced with one another in a slow and graceful motion, unaware of the challenge at hand in their water world. Alison kicked hard and thrust herself back to the surface. Her right leg nicked the protruding jagged lava rock, causing her to bleed instantly. Sharks began to circle to the left of where Casey had been bitten. She immediately sensed blood in the water and pushed on towards the surface. Alison had been underwater for almost thirty seconds without a breath. As she neared the surface, she could see the Tiger Sharks circling with purpose. *Pull, kick, pull, kick*, she thought to herself as she pushed on.

"Ah!" she gasped as her head rose above the surface. Stopping for a brief moment, she plunged her face into the water to look for sharks. Alison took a large breath and started to swim for the shore.

"She is on the other side," said Mr. Y calmly.

"She is?" asked Tony, almost in disbelief. "Go Alison!" he yelled with his hands shaped around his mouth to project the sound towards her. The sharks closed in with speed and precision, outmatching the speed maintained by Alison. As she neared the beach, she could see the sand just below her, knowing that the depth was only four or five feet. *Almost there.* Just then, a shark bumped into her right leg, testing its prey. The water was now only three feet deep and Alison stood up and started to wade towards the beach.

"Son-of-a-bitch!" she called out as the watery run prevented her from moving rapidly. "Twenty more feet," she gasped. She had made it past the sharks! She ran up the wet sand towards the white line. She pumped her arms as hard as they would go, fists clenched tightly. At the line, she dove onto the beach. "Oh my God," she gasped, rolling over to her back, her bleeding leg and part of her chest exposed as the bikini top slipped off during her dive to the ground.

"Tony!" she screamed with all her strength. "You can make it!" she continued, verbally and physically exhausted. Tony could hear her from a distance and called back to her.

"Alison! Are you alright?"

"Sorry Ms. Watson," stated Mr. Y, as he hovered near Tony. "Just over two minutes," he continued. He reset his trusty stopwatch. *Snap*. She was gone.

"Shit!" called out Tony. "Where is she? Let me talk to her," he demanded. "How do you know she didn't make it in time? You weren't even on the other side."

"Sorry, Mr. Blackwell. For what it is worth, she was close. Take that into consideration before you decide which way you go," he continued. "Ready?"

"You son-of-a-bitch."

"Ready?" groaned Mr. Y.

"Please. Anger will get you nowhere with me Mr. Blackwell. Take it out on your challenge," he commanded as he raised the stopwatch. "Three, two, one, go!"

Dream Challenge

Tony dove over the boat's railing into the water and raced directly towards the rock ahead of him. Sharks with blood in the water made the challenge difficult. *Do it in one breath*, he thought as he expertly maneuvered himself on top of the water with a freestyle stroke. *Breath. Get this under control,* he thought. Within thirty seconds, he was close to the rock. Instead of swimming under it as Alison had done, he climbed out of the water and started to hike over it, thinking that it would save him time. The black lava rock was sharp and cut into his feet with each step he took across the rocky beast.

Mr. Y smiled at his tenacity, eyes on the stopwatch. Using his hands, Tony continued to climb the rocks until he reached the top, briefly turning back to look at his host and flip him the middle finger. Mr. Y just smiled and stayed focused, slowly bobbing up and down above the deck in an effortless levitation, stopwatch in hand. As Tony climbed down the other side of the rock, he could see the white line clearly on the beach. Two torches burned, positioned on either side of the white line, and served as a goal post for the finish line. He could see sharks in the near distance circling where Alison surfaced after her swim under the rock. Tony moved slightly to the right, away from the fish.

"Thirty yards," muttered Tony as he re-entered the water. *You can do it Blackwell.* He dove into the surf, arms outstretched and hands clasped together like clamshells to optimize his swim. *Faster, faster*, thought Tony as he raced towards the beach, swimming a little wider to the right to get away from the sharks.

Within moments, the sharks changed direction and swam towards Tony. Still underwater, they honed in on their prey. *Faster!* Tony pulled and kicked as fast as he could, rapidly approaching the shoreline. As he did so, blood trickled into the sea from the bottom of his feet. He left a trail for the sharks. In between breaths, he saw a shark directly below him. *Fifteen yards,* he thought. *Pull, pull!* As he kept his eyes on the shark below, Tony didn't see the one coming at him from behind. The shark quickly closed in on Tony.

"Shit!" barked Tony as a shark blindsided him and slammed into his legs. Tony stopped swimming for an instant to take an inventory of the sharks around him. He treaded water and spun around three hundred and sixty degrees to see how many sharks were around him. "Crap! They are all around me," he yelled aloud. Tony had no choice but to swim for the shore as fast as he could. The group of fish coordinated a second attack. Slam! Another shark rammed Tony from the left side, causing him to take in water. He stopped again to tread water and stayed afloat within the circling sharks.

"Ouch!" yelled Tony as a shark bit into his left leg from below. Blood started to fill the water. The sharks intensified their attack. Several of them nipped at Tony's legs.

"Somebody help me!" he screamed. Mr. Y focused on the stopwatch as it counted down to two minutes. Tony could now see multiple dorsal fins circling him. His heart raced as he started to panic. Slam! A shark hit his right side, causing Tony to take in seawater. The pain became intense, from his ribs to cuts on his feet and leg. Coughing and still attempting to swim, Tony pressed towards the shore. Faster, faster!

"Three, two, one," counted Mr. Y calmly, now hovering over the beach just past the finish line. "You are done, Mr. Blackwell" *Snap!*

15 – CENTERS FOR DISEASE CONTROL AND PREVENTION

Alison Watson jolted up to a sitting position in her bed and woke from her dream.

"Holy cow," she exhaled and recognized that she had just failed another dream challenge. *I wonder if Tony made it.* Exhausted and famished, she headed to the kitchen and poured herself a bowl of cereal and milk. The laptop was still running and connected to the Internet. Alison moved from the kitchen, cereal in tow, to the family room. Staring at the computer and wanting to know, but not wanting at the same time, she put her hands on the keyboard. *Does he exist?* She typed the phrase into the search engine's keyword text box.

Keyword Search: *"Tony Blackwell"*

Results: *29,204*

Twenty-nine thousand links? She closed the window and folded the laptop screen down.

"I don't want to know," she whispered as she turned on the television and browsed for something interesting to watch.

* * *

Tony sat up and gasped, quickly pulling the bed sheets off him and looking down at his legs. He was still badly bruised, but no blood. He grabbed one foot and turned it towards his face so that he could see the bottom. There appeared to be no cuts from the coral.

"This thing is killing me," he stated, trying to gain control of his breathing and heart rate.

It was 5:00 a.m. After realizing that the video system was still recording, Tony promptly ripped off the rubber connections from his chest, stood up, walked over to the machine, and promptly turned it off. "No more recordings," he stated, then returned to the bed to lie down. With his arms behind his head and ankles now crossed, he pondered the most recent dream. *Did I really kiss Alison? Holy crap. It was actually nice and I think she liked it.*

"What is happening to me? How in hell can I be falling for a girl that doesn't exist?" stated Tony. He sprang out of bed and walked out of the recording room. The nurse at the duty station quickly took notice.

"Mr. Blackwell, can I help you? Do you need something?"

"No, I'm fine. I just need to walk a bit. It's too cramped in that room if you know what I mean," continued Tony. The nurse simply nodded. "I will be in the hallway if you need me," stated Tony as he walked past the woman, bare-chested and bruised, pajama pants skimming the cold white floor.

Dream Challenge

* * *

Dr. Richard Lewis stood outside Peter Smith's office. The office door was closed. The physician impatiently looked at his watch for the fourth or fifth time. As he did so, Dr. Smith rounded the corner and pulled out his keys to unlock his office door.

"Can I help you?"

"Yes. I am Dr. Richard Lewis with the CDC. We need to talk," he returned bluntly and without emotion.

"Ok? Come on in and have a seat. I will be right with you," said the physician as he opened the door.

"Dr. Smith. We need a private place to talk. Not here. Walk with me," responded Dr. Lewis. Confused, but interested in what the man had to say, Peter Smith placed his patient folders on the counter, asked the nurse to file them, and turned to follow the CDC man out the entrance to his office.

"Where are we going?"

"Outside," responded Lewis as he strode slightly ahead of the Mass General doctor. Within minutes, the two men were outside of the hospital and walking down a side street. "What I am about to tell you is classified for your ears only. Over the last few months, we have tracked some strange patient symptoms that came in from all around the world. At the end of a painful cycle, each patient eventually died, usually within five to seven days. I believe that your patient – Mr. Tony Blackwell, will also die within the coming two to three days unless we can figure out what's causing his symptoms." Peter Smith walked alongside the CDC man with a concerned look on his face.

"How many patients have had these types of symptoms?"

"One hundred and thirty-four. All dead," Lewis responded. Peter Smith stopped walking.

"Are we dealing with an epidemic Doctor?"

"No, not yet."

"What's the cause of this? Bird Flu, Ebola, Dengue?"

"No. All the patients tested came up negative. We simply don't know what's causing this, but the numbers are rising. Listen, I'm going to need a blood sample from Mr. Blackwell."

"Sure, but why?"

"I need to run some tests against a few of the most dangerous viruses on Earth."

"Which ones?" stated Dr. Smith.

"That, my dear colleague, is classified information. Sorry," continued Dr. Lewis. *God, I hope this is not the military 322 strain,* he thought.

"Classified? What the hell is going on here Doctor?"

"Again, I'm sorry I can't elaborate," replied the CDC expert. "This investigation is classified Top Secret."

* * *

Later in the day, Alison dialed her friend at work.

"Rachel, it's me. Can you talk?"

"Yes. I'm just finishing up a presentation for Susie on the collaboration suite updates and getting ready to go to lunch."

"I had another one of those dreams last night," stated Alison. She proceeded to tell her friend about the recent dream. "I thought I was going to die. Sharks were nipping at my legs as I swam," she continued, the details still fresh in her mind. "There was a new contestant in the dream too. Casey Wilson was his name," stated Alison. He was a real meat head, you know? The kind of guy who'd wear a tight tank top at spring break in Daytona, Florida and be sloppy drunk all week."

"Alison. I think you should see someone about these dreams,"suggested Rachel.

"What, like a doctor?"

"Yes."

"Forget it. I am not crazy Rachel. As real as these things seem, they're *not* real," barked Alison into the phone.

"Then tell me why you get the physical symptoms you get when you dream?" replied Rachel. Alison paused.

"I have to go. Do not tell anybody about this!" she commanded, then promptly hung up the phone. *Am I going crazy?*

* * *

"Mr. Blackwell. I'm going to need another blood sample," stated Dr. Smith.

"What for?"

"We are just going to run some additional tests to rule out a few things."

"Like what?"

"Don't worry Tony. If I find something, you will be the first to know," stated Dr. Smith. "I promise. I'm here to help and have a team working hard to find the root cause of your symptoms so that we can appropriately treat you," continued Dr. Smith. "The nurse will be in soon to draw your blood."

"What about the most recent test on my stomach and intestines?" asked Tony.

"The scope came up negative," replied the physician. "Your digestive track was clear and we found no indication of ulcers in the lining of your stomach either," replied Dr. Smith.

"That's a good thing, right?"

"Yes, it is Tony," stated Dr. Smith. "Oh yeah, I'd like to run the EEG, one more time tonight while you dream if that's ok with you?"asked Dr. Smith

"Nope. I'm done with that test," shot back Tony, arms folded defiantly across his chest. Dr. Smith froze and looked at his patient. Tony was bruised and clearly in pain. Understanding Tony's frustration, Dr. Smith simply nodded, then walked out of the room. His patient needed some time to rest.

* * *

Anya Kuzma set up her equipment in an apartment within range of Casey Wilson's house. She started the program and configured it to send and receive signals to the recently planted device. As she waited, Kuzma turned on the television and turned the channel to Fox News. The news anchor reported the daily news in traditional American boisterous fashion.

"Such pigs," stated Anya. "American pigs," she continued, her disdain clear for the land of the free.

16 – A KNIGHT'S ARMOR

Casey, Tony, and Alison all stood inside a padded white room. Cool air gushed from the ceiling through small pores in the tiles. A cloudy froth rained down on top of the competitors. There were no obvious exits in the room. All three contestants looked around to take in their surroundings, then at each other.

"Here we are again," mused Casey, who instantly began inspecting the walls for a hidden exit. He tested various points with pressure to find a secreted opening.

"Hey cutie, want to help me?" called out Casey towards Alison.

"Leave her alone," responded Tony sternly, who walked straight towards Alison.

"Hey Tony. I guess you didn't make it either," stated Alison.

"I could hear you from the other side," replied Tony as he moved closer towards her. "Thanks for trying to warn me, but don't do it again," he whispered.

"Why not?" replied Alison as she took Tony's hand and pulled him closer.

"I can't tell you, but just *don't*. Trust me," he replied softly. Tony glanced at Casey, who was still searching for an exit. "I'm really starting to dislike that guy," he said, staring directly at the large muscular man. "Who names their baby boy Casey anyway?" he mused. "No wonder he's such an idiot," continued Tony, still staring at the large injudicious adult. "I guess we should help him figure a way out of here though, right?"

The pair joined Casey, where the three oddly related contestants poked and prodded the walls and floor to find a way out of the psycho-looking room. Each of the contestants appeared relaxed as they worked in silence. Their clothing exposed a window into each person's habits, personality, and potentially their geographical home in real life. Tony paid attention to his surroundings more than most. Alison wore a short sleeve sport shirt, a pair of tan shorts that stopped six inches above her knees, and a pair of leather open sandals, showcasing her French manicured toes.

Casey wore a classic bar-wear outfit. His distressed and slightly ripped tight fitting tee shirt was adorned with a crude drinking slogan. The shirt complemented a pair of full-length bright yellow swim shorts. Finally, checkered sneakers with the laces undone sheltered his feet. Tony was dressed in a simple long-sleeve Oxford collared shirt, sleeves rolled up to the elbow, a pair of khaki pants, and expensive looking leather loafers.

"Hey, I think I found something," said Casey as he tried to pry the puffy padding apart through what appeared to be an open seam. The others gathered around for a closer inspection.

"What have you found Mr. Wilson?" called Mr. Y from across the room. The stunned group all turned around to see Mr. Y hovering in front of an open door. The opening showed a clear blue space beyond the frame. As Tony stared at the host, he saw what appeared to be a distant cloud passing behind Mr. Y at a slow, but steady pace. *How can that be?* he thought.

"Dude, I've had just about enough of this," replied Casey as he turned to walk towards the host. Mr. Y instinctively shook his head. Casey froze instantly, eyes wide open in shock, unable to move or talk. With a flip of Mr. Y's head to the left, Casey's body flew through the air until it slammed into the wall and collapsed to the floor.

"God, I love padded walls," commented the host with a smile on his face. "Ok, now back to business. Tonight, I am going to let one of you decide where and what we do with our challenge. Please all gather in the middle of the room and close your eyes," he continued. Alison and Tony held hands and moved to the center of the room as ordered. "You too Mr. Wilson, unless you'd rather not play tonight." Casey picked himself up off the floor, muttered an unintelligible phrase, and reluctantly met the others in the center of the room.

"Now, all of you gently close your eyes and free your minds," instructed Mr. Y with one of the most soothing voices the group had ever heard. Within moments, Tony's stressful expression was gone and replaced with a look of Zen and comfort. Alison also complied and when she reached a full state of meditation, she unknowingly released Tony's hand. Casey, however, rocked back and forth with pursed lips, still smarting from his brief scuffle with Mr. Y.

"I want each of you to think of yourself as a warrior, in any time, place, or period. The first one to have a clear image will be the winner," he continued as if he were conducting a group hypnotherapy session. Five seconds passed with pure silence. "That's it, someone's getting close," he whispered, anticipation in his voice.

"Ding, ding, ding! We have a winner. Johnny, tell them what they've won," called out Mr. Y, with hands outstretched, palms and eyes toward the ceiling.

"I didn't think of anything. Who did?" called out Casey angrily. Alison opened her eyes and turned to look at Tony, whose eyes were still shut.

"Tony, what did you do?" asked Alison softly. "What did you think of?"

"You don't want to know," he replied, eyes now opened and staring intensely at the evening's peculiar host. Mr. Y raised his right hand and pressed his index finger and thumb together.

"Don't do it!" called out Casey, but it was too late. *Snap!*

Instantly, the trio stood in a lush green field in between surrounding mountains. Several ancient castles were visible in the distance on opposite hills.

"Where are we?" asked Alison, as she gazed at her surroundings.

"We are in England my dear," replied Mr. Y, hovering just to her left. "Thirteenth century I believe, isn't that right Mr. Blackwell?"

"Tony, what are we doing here? What did you do?" asked Alison, with a concerned expression on her face.

"Conflictus Gallicus, Ms. Watson. Conflictus Gallicus. My dear, we have been granted a license for tournament by no other than King Richard the Lionheart," beamed Mr. Y. "What a glorious day, wouldn't you all agree? Now that we are here, you'll each get to choose a weapon, which will determine your challenge."

"What weapons?" asked Tony.

"Your choices include a sword, a lance, or a bow and arrow," returned Mr. Y.

"What are the tournament games?" asked Alison.

"In due time, my dear. In due time," responded the host. Alison and Tony huddled to discuss their options, when Casey blurted out his preference.

"I'll take the lance, man. Seems really cool." Tony and Alison whispered for a few moments, before turning towards Mr. Y. After acknowledging each other with a simple head nod, Tony selected their weapons.

"I'll take the sword, and Alison will have the bow and arrow," stated Tony.

"Excellent choices," returned Mr. Y with a satisfied look on his face. *Snap!*

Instantly, hundreds of cheering English fans lined a variety of venues, each roped off to keep the spectators out of harm's way. Several fires burned in the distance. Some of the English prepared meals in large iron pots that hung above the glowing fire pits. Torches on long, thin wooden poles burned across the land, encircling each tournament venue.

"Whoa," stated Casey, as he took in the environment around him. "This is going to be great!" he continued, now wearing a full coat of armor, complete with a tailor-made series of chain mail and iron plates. Sabatons, greaves, poleyns, and cuisses armor covered his legs. Rerebrace to vambrace covered his arms, while a black-colored chest and back plate of armor protected his midsection. A full bascinet helmet with a skirt of mail protected his head and neck.

The visor, still open, allowed the medieval knight's face to be visible to the spectators. Casey Wilson raised a shield towards the sky, showcasing his coat of arms. The crowd roared in approval. Sir Wilson, satisfied with the response, merely smiled.

Casey's white coat of armor included a diagonal green line. On either side of the line, were two dominant red crosses. As tradition would hold for this era of warrior, a dagger and sword hung from Casey's belt. A beautiful black stallion stood next to Casey, snorting with anticipation as if he knew what was about to happen. The magnificent beast was adorned with a matching green and white cloth draped across his back and around his chest. The gray sky swirled slowly as the clouds seemed to dance with one another. Patches of ground level fog rose from the cold and wet Earth, seeming to reach towards the sky.

After focusing on Casey, Alison and Tony each looked at their tournament attire. Alison wore a traditional cloth archer uniform, complete with a black long sleeve shirt and a cape that fit over her head and traversed down to her knees. The red cape, adorned with four bold white crosses, was held tight with a matching white cloth belt. Brown leather boots laced twelve inches up her calves protected her from the wet and soggy English countryside.

Tony, also wearing knight's armor, sported a different coat of arms. His coat was solid black, with white lines splitting the center of the shield both horizontally and vertically. On the top left and bottom right sections, large red stars were visible. On opposite sides of the lines, white swords formed a diagonal cross, highlighting that the knight who wore it, was in fact a swordsman. Tony's right hand firmly grasped a long and heavy iron sword. After pointing the iron towards the sky, he turned and plunged the sword into the ground, causing it to vibrate back and forth. The crowd erupted in cheers. Tony opened his visor to see more clearly and gazed at the crowd, before turning towards Alison.

"Listen to me. Just remember to win," he said softly. "Just win. Don't think of anything else when it's your turn, ok?"

"Ok. By the way, you look really handsome in that outfit Sir Blackwell," she joked, bow held firmly in her left hand, quiver full of colorful arrows comfortably resting on her back.

"I'm serious, Alison. Do *not* be fooled by any of this. It doesn't exist!" he said before regaining a whispering tone. "It's not real," he continued, pointing around the English countryside.

Just then, the trumpets began their cry. The performers played their notes in unison, from low to high and back again, as the festivities got underway.

"Ladies and gentlemen, the first event of the day will be a joust between Sir Wilson and the Black Knight of Warwick!" called the announcer.

"Sir Wilson. You are up," calmly stated Mr. Y. "You will be jousting an experienced knight, so pay attention. The first to knock his opponent off their horse, wins. You must abide by the rules of the tournament and only pass to the right side of your approaching opponent. You'll have as many passes as it takes until we have a winner," continued Mr. Y. "Good luck."

"What, no stopwatch tonight?" mused Casey, who mounted his stallion and took the reins.

"Funny, Mr. Wilson," replied Mr. Y as he snapped his fingers. A long blunt-ended lance, commonly used in the thirteenth century by decree from King Edward I via the Statute of Arms in 1292, was now firmly in Casey's grip. "You can knock your opponent off his horse with the lance, but it likely won't kill him," stated the host.

"Knights. Mount your horses and move to the starting location!" called the announcer. Casey directed his steed towards the jousting area. As his stallion galloped towards the starting point, he raised the lance into the air, causing an instant response from the crowd. Casey circled his horse and surveyed the crowd as he neared the end of the centerline separating the two paths each knight would ride between.

Cheering fans wore cloth coat of arms from both knights. More English appeared to be showing their preference towards the Black Knight of Warwick. This didn't dissuade Casey. He pulled back on the reigns, causing his horse to rise up and stand on two legs. Mr. Y smiled at the stunt. Tony shook his head in disgust, as he and Alison stood as temporary spectators to the show.

"Riders, take your positions!" called the announcer. Each rider complied. Bobbing slightly on his steed, the Black Knight of

Warwick stared at his opponent from across the fifty-yard field. Signaling he was ready, the knight lowered his visor and raised his lance to a thirty-degree angle towards the sky. Casey responded with the same actions. "Begin!" yelled the host of the event.

Both horses galloped on their appropriate sides towards one another, each gaining in speed as they neared the center of the field. The Black Knight lowered his lance to a horizontal position as he achieved an optimum speed. As the two brave knights passed one another, each attempted a deadly blow at the other. Their lances clashed, but prevented bodily contact. The crowd erupted in applause. As the two riders regrouped on their opposite sides, both horses circled while their riders displayed their lances towards the sky. This was done to rest their arms from the weight of holding the heavy lances forward during battle. Casey flipped up his visor and stared directly at his opponent.

The crowd responded with boos as they showed their allegiance to their preferred knight. In response, Casey lowered his visor and began to gallop towards the Black Knight, staying just to the right of the divider. The Knight of Warwick responded with an even faster run towards Sir Wilson. As the pair of knights neared the center of the field, each lowered their lance and assumed attack positions. Just before the knights clashed, Casey leaned to the right, and lowered his lance, causing it to strike the Black Knight on the leg. The crowd went wild as the underdog drew first blood with a body strike.

Alison and Tony watched from the sidelines and wondered about their respective contests and fate. As each knight regrouped from the second pass, the applause from the crowd only rose. Angry spectators could be heard predicting Sir Wilson the jousting loser. Currently, Sir Wilson was winning the match. Thrusting his lance into the air, Casey turned and directed his horse to gallop again towards his opponent. The Black Knight of Warwick reciprocated and began to move his steed down the now worn path with increasing speed. As the pair of knights gained speed and lowered their lances, the crowd's applause grew. The synchronous sound of hoofs thumped the ground as the fans cheered.

As the two knights approached one another, the Black Knight began to move his lance in a circular motion, confusing Casey. As they met, the expert from Warwick centered his lance and struck Casey with a direct hit to the left hip, spinning him around and easily knocking him off his horse. The crowd exploded in applause and chants in support of the Black Knight.

The victorious Black Knight rode his steed past the crowd. A very skilled knight had beaten Casey Wilson. Alison and Tony stared ahead as Casey attempted to get up from the ground. He was definitely injured from the lance's blow. Alison moved forward to help, but Tony held her back.

"No, Alison! He'll be gone in a moment," said Tony. *Snap!*

Instantly, the jousting tournament was replaced by a series of stone walls, stacked ten feet high, two feet wide, and ten feet long, positioned in the shape of triangles. Casey and the Black Knight were gone. Three foot paths between each stone wall allowed for human passage between the man-made structures.

"Ladies and gentleman. Please take your places around the archery section as we move to our next event," called the announcer.

"Ms. Watson, this one is actually quite simple," whispered Mr. Y. "You just need to stay alive and shoot your opponent first, before they shoot you," he continued, hovering slightly above the grassy field. Tony stood on the sideline with the rest of the spectators. He could see Alison and Mr. Y through gaps in the stones, but could not hear what they were saying.

"Alison, be careful!" yelled Tony, only to be drowned out by the crowd's cheers.

"Today's match will be between archers Ms. Alison Watson and the beautiful Princess of York," he continued. The crowd erupted in support.

"York, York, York." Tony looked around at the growing crowd and approached one of the other spectators.

"Is the princess a good archer?"

"Why of course, my friend. She's one of the best in the land and the only royal, brave enough to fight," replied the man. "I've got fifteen pence on her my friend," he continued, then took a swig of ale from his battered pewter mug.

"Great," murmured Tony. All he could do now was watch and hope. Trumpets erupted in unison to lead the fanfare and instructions before the match.

"Thank you, thank you," stated the host. "In this event, each archer will start out on opposite sides of the rock formations. Once the event starts, each contestant must remain within the confines of the tournament's space, but can use the stone walls as they see fit. The match ends when one of the archers is struck by the other's arrow, to be confirmed with the arrow still in their body," he completed. The crowd roared with support.

"Good luck Ms. Watson," said Mr. Y, who with a snap, disappeared from within the rock structures and re-appeared next to Tony Blackwell.

"Archers, please take your places!" called the announcer. The princess emerged from a crowd of supporters, flanked by members of the Royal Army. Wearing a white cape, complete with York's coat of arms prominently displayed on the front, the

Princess of York entered the confines of the event. Cleared of the ropes, she proceeded as instructed to the outside edge of the oddly shaped rock structures. Indicating she was ready, the Princess of York drew an arrow from her quiver, loaded it into her waiting bow, and raised the bow into the air above the landscape. The crowd exploded in applause.

Alison passed through one of the gaps in the rocks and assumed her position opposite the princess. She nodded to the announcer and acknowledged that she was ready. The announcer, who sat on top of the middle rock formation, had a clear view of both contestants. He lowered his arms and waved colorful flags, indicating that the event had commenced.

The princess and Alison both slowly gravitated towards the middle stone structure. They each weaved in and out of the gaps between the tall rock formations, looking for a clear glimpse of their opponent.

Alison retrieved an arrow from her quiver and positioned it, ready to fire. Standing still, she peered around a wall and spotted the Princess of York. Excited, Alison attempted to move closer. The princess countered her opponents approach and doubled back around the stone structure. The Princess of York spotted Ms. Watson as she cautiously moved through the outer edges of the rock formation. Quietly, she pulled the bowstring back, aimed, and fired. The arrow swooshed through the air silently and careened off a rock just above Alison's head.

"York, York, York, York," cheered the crowd in support of the popular princess. The slight wind caused the arrow to miss its target. The princess would likely not make the same mistake twice. Torches burned around the event's borders. The crowd suddenly got quiet as they waited to see how the archers would again stalk one another.

Alison stayed on the outside of the rocks and moved south towards the base of the southern-most triangle. The princess quietly tore off a portion of her uniform and held it firmly in her hand as she moved north towards the tip of a triangle in the middle of the arena.

Each archer weaved silently between the rocks, stalking the other. Alison positioned herself at the base of a triangle, readied her arrow to fire, and waited for the princess to show herself. As the Princess of York passed along the outer edge of the rock, Alison readied a shot. Left eye closed, she released the deadly arrow towards the royal archer. The arrow flew quietly across the field, but hit just behind her target. The crowd gasped at the closeness of the shot and returned to silence. Tony just stood and watched as the event unfolded.

"Dammit," whispered Alison. She knew that she had to lead her target due to the time it took the arrow to travel the distance across the field. She turned left at the base of the structure and began to move east. As the princess passed the top of the triangle's point, Alison stuffed a torn portion of her garment into a crevice in the rocky wall. The wind, blowing east, caused the garment to dangle in the wind, occasionally pushing the outer edge of the cloth past the outside edge of the wall.

Looking before each movement, the princess moved left and then southwest. Demonstrating her superiority and skill, the Princess of York, timed each movement between the gaps so that her opponent could not see her. Alison continued east until she reached the bottom right edge of the triangle. As she peered around the corner, she noticed a cloth garment peering out from the outer edge of the wall. She moved slowly north as she stalked her prey. An arrow at the ready, Alison carefully took steps forward.

"Now I've got you," stated Alison quietly, sensing that the princess was positioned still for a shot at her approaching from the west. Alison continued to move closer towards her prey. The crowd was silent. All that could be heard were the torches flickering in the English countryside wind.

Twenty feet before the garment, Alison carefully moved to the path between the rocks and placed her back against the wall. After pausing for almost five seconds, she slowly peered to the north along the inside edge of the wall. Looking for a shot that would surprise the princess, Alison drew her arrow back and waited.

Just poke your little head out. I know you're there, she thought. With her right eye on the targeted space and the left closed to ensure accuracy, she waited.

"Shit!" yelled Alison unexpectedly, as an arrow pierced through her left shoulder. The crowd erupted in applause as the Princess of York came out from hiding. She had also left a piece of her outfit on the wall to attract her opponent. Alison dropped her bow, collapsed to one knee in pain, and grasped her wound. Blood spewed from her shoulder in an uncontrolled manner.

"Alison!" shouted Tony as he ran towards her. "Alison!" *Snap.* Instantly she was gone, as was the archery venue and tournament. Tony stopped running and realized that he was standing in a roped off rocky portion of the English countryside. Spectators leaned up against the ropes and chanted for the match to begin. Mr. Y hovered next to Tony, but was invisible to the English crowd.

"Now it's your turn, Sir Blackwell. You will be fighting an experienced knight with your sword. You may use your dagger if you see fit, as the fight will be to the death," he continued. "The only way you can get your blade through the knight's armor is through the thin layer of chain mail. Of course, if you remove his helmet, you can simply slit his throat," he continued, chuckling.

"I don't want to slit his throat or anybody else's throat," cried out Tony. "I want to get out of this place," he continued. "Now!"

"Well, Sir Blackwell, if you leave, you fail, and your track record isn't the best lately," gloated Mr. Y. "If you stay, however, I guarantee you that your opponent will stop at nothing to kill you, so you better be prepared." *Snap*. Mr. Y vanished.

"This is bullshit!" shouted Tony. Tony experimented with the weight of his iron sword. He looked over his armor adorned with a solid black and white lined coat of arms and briefly wondered about its history.

"Ladies and gentlemen. May I draw your attention to the last event of our fine tournament. A duel to the finish," proclaimed the announcer. The crowd cheered loudly, more so than for any other event. Ale flowed freely and sloshed within the patron's mugs. There were quite intoxicated and becoming unruly.

"Cut his heart out!" shouted one man. The intoxicated crowd cheered in support, with several men and women yelling additional suggestions.

"Kill the visitor!"

"Cut his heart out, then his balls off!"

"Now, now," stated the announcer. "Let's give our visitor a fighting chance, yes?"

"Hell no!"

"Send him home in a box," yelled another.

"Ladies and gentlemen. Please," asked the announcer, briefly calming the rowdy crowd. "To my left is Sir Blackwell, the Gentle," said the announcer, nodding towards Tony. "And to my right is Sir Longworth of Berkshire," he continued. The crowd roared in support of the local hero. "Gentlemen, this is a fight to the death. The only rule is that you must stay within the confines of the fighting area. Other than that, there are *no* other rules," he continued. "Are you both ready?" Tony and the other knight nodded, lowered their visors, and raised their shields. "Commence!" called the announcer as he quickly moved away from the men in armor to avoid harm's way.

The two warriors moved cautiously in a circular motion. Each eyed the other through the thin gaps in their visors. Sir Longworth struck first, swinging his heavy sword from the side at Tony's midsection. Tony's sword intercepted the strike as he positioned the blade towards the ground in a blocking fashion. The spectators cheered and raised their mugs of ale in support of the visiting knight. The pair of warriors continued their odd dance, moving as gracefully as they could with the heavy weight of the armor limiting their speed and motion. Tony swung next. Using two hands to grasp the sword, he swung the blade top-down towards the other knight's head.

"Whoa!" responded the crowd, as Sir Longworth moved to the left just before the blade struck the ground. Tony stumbled forward as his sword rebounded off the English soil. Sir Longworth took advantage of the opportunity and struck Sir Blackwell with the base of his sword across the head. Tony was knocked off balance, but not down. The crowd responded with a coordinated roar of support.

"Long live Sir Longworth. Long live Sir Longworth."

Tony quickly gained his footing and again moved in a circular motion directly across from his adversary. Longworth swung again. *Crash!* The blade slammed into Tony's shield. Tony breathed heavy and his heart raced. Clearly outmatched, he needed to figure out a way to surprise the able-bodied knight. *Crash!* Sir Longworth struck another blow, this time glancing Tony's armor plated shoulder. The metal on metal clank was rewarded by cheers from the unruly spectators, now chanting with arms outstretched towards the sky.

"Longworth, Longworth!"

"Shit," gasped Tony, as he regrouped from the painful blow. *Think outside the box.* In a surprise display of talent, Tony moved forward and lunged his weapon at the midsection of the opposing knight. The crowd replied with a gasp. Sir Longworth, seemingly not phased, stepped to the side, placed his foot past Tony, and knocked his opponent to the ground. Immediately, Tony knew that he was in trouble. The weight of the suit prevented him from getting up quickly. Sir Longworth moved in for the kill. While lying on his back, Tony attempted to swing his sword from the side to defend himself, but his skilled opponent merely knocked it from his hands and to the ground with a powerful counter swing.

"Prepare to die," called out Longworth as he stood over Tony, sword leveled directly at his throat.

"Wait, Sir Longworth!" asked Tony, but the knight did not pause. Instead, Sir Longworth drove his sword through the thin chain mail protecting Tony's neck and into his opponent's throat. The crowd erupted in cheers.

The winning knight moved in for a closer look. The crowd grew silent in response. Now kneeling, Sir Longworth opened the enemy's visor to see his opponent's face. Tony's eyes were wide open in shock. He repeatedly gasped for air. Sir Longworth just stared into Tony's eyes with no emotion. Longworth's sword stood vertically on its own, through Tony's neck and into the ground below. The countryside wind moved the sword gently from side to side. The crowd just stared in awe. *Snap!*

* * *

Tony immediately sat up and pulled the sheets off his chest. Covered in sweat and heart racing, he cupped both hands around his throat.

"Goddammit," he exhaled, realizing his throat was intact. "When will this shit stop?" The heart monitor pulsed synchronously as the video recorder silently documented the event for Dr. Smith. Tony sat alone trying to regain control over his erratic breathing.

17 – THE LIGHT AT THE END OF THE TUNNEL

Casey Wilson woke up in a sweat, now sitting upright in bed. A young woman adorned with cheap tattoos rolled over next to him, the white sheet contouring along her shapely and full-figured body.

"What is wrong?" she questioned, her eyes barely open.

"Nothing. I am fine," replied Casey, now looking at the clock. It was 5:30 a.m. on Wednesday morning. He had to be on the construction site by 7:00 a.m.

"Go back to bed," whispered the woman as she curled up next to him, pulling the covers up over her green and yellow butterfly tattoo on the back of her neck. Casey smiled. He liked fast women with cheap tattoos, and reminisced about meeting her last night at TJ's bar. Knowing he couldn't sleep and with the dream still fresh in his mind, he quietly slid out of the bed. His new conquest just groaned and rolled back to the other side of the mattress.

Casey walked into the kitchen and turned on the small television sitting on the counter. Music videos played in the background as he prepared something to eat. Reaching to the cabinet for a bowl, he growled.

"Ouch, that's painful," he said, looking at the outer part of his left triceps. "I don't remember that bruise," he mused aloud. "Man, that must have been some great sex last night." Empty beer bottles and spent candle wax littered the den. As Casey Wilson poured cereal into a bowl, the sun started to rise above the flat Florida horizon. In thirty minutes, he would have to wake up the woman in his bed and kick her out of his apartment. Smiling, he watched the sunrise out the window and ate his breakfast.

* * *

Dr. Peter Smith, at the request of the CDC, had moved Tony to a quarantined portion of the hospital. The room was equipped with its own ventilation system to keep any contaminants from getting in or out. Tony's condition was getting worse. His bruises continued to expand in number and darkened in color. After each night's sleep, Tony bled from his nose or through urine that he expelled at the start of each day. Doctors from the hospital and CDC huddled in a war room nearby.

"I am telling you Peter, we may just have to make a public statement if this thing gets any more out of control," stated Richard Lewis, pointing his pen at the Mass General physician.

"We don't even know what this young kid has Richard," shot back Smith. "He has come up clean on every test we've run." Richard Lewis's ultra secure Boeing Black cell phone buzzed.

"Excuse me," said Lewis, moving to the outer edges of the room for a bit of privacy. "Lewis here. What is it?"

"We got another notice this morning from Beijing," stated the man on the other line. "That brings us to one hundred and thirty-five," he continued. Dr. Lewis paused.

"Are we still on for that call this afternoon?"asked the CDC expert.

"Yes. You will need to go back to the military installation to take the call. It must be secure."

"Ok. Thanks," responded Lewis as he hung up the phone and re-joined the debate in the middle of the room.

"Listen, gentlemen. Dr. Smith, I think we need to prepare the patient for what looks like the inevitable. Make him comfortable," suggested the CDC man, secure phone still in his hand.

"Who was that on the phone?" asked one of the men in the room.

"We had another death last night with identical symptoms to what Mr. Blackwell is exhibiting."

* * *

Colonel Jones hung up the phone. The test results were ready. He walked out of his office and turned right. He continued down a long hallway that descended into the ground at a gradual, but steady slope. Seventy-five feet later, he came to a steel door with a passcode and a biometric sensor. Reggie Jones entered a seven-digit code and placed his palm on the flat panel sensor. The scanner took an image of his five fingerprints, and after matching them against a small list of approved images, unlocked the door. Colonel Jones pulled the large, heavy door open and passed through the archway. Inside, were a series of scientists busily working, and a layer of rooms that went from traditional to clean.

"Colonel Jones, I have your report," called out the young Army specialist.

"Has this been verified by Dr. Levinson?"

"Yes, sir. Would you like to speak to her?"

"No. That will be all," stated Colonel Jones, as he turned left and headed down the hall to a vacant room. He wanted to review the newly prepared report in private. As he closed the door, the cramped and windowless office came into full view. Reggie sat down and opened the folder. The document was stamped in red with the phrase *top-secret* that included a surrounding rectangular red box.

"Let's see what we have here," spoke the Colonel aloud as he settled into the chair. After scanning the introductory text, he flipped to page three, where he focused on the result.

"Oh my God," he uttered, before placing the opened report on the table in front of him. "God help us all," he continued.

* * *

The secretary of the U.S. Department of Health and Human Services called the conference call to order.

"Ladies and gentlemen. Thank you for coming together on such short notice.

Richard, can you provide us with an update please?" politely asked Jules Mitchell.

"Thank you, Madam Secretary. At this point, we know of one hundred and thirty-five cases across the globe. They were reported over the last six months. All of the patients exhibited similar rapidly degrading conditions, and eventually expired due to internal bleeding," stated the CDC point person.

"Did any of the tests performed come up positive for Dengue or Ebola?" asked the National Security Advisor.

"No, they did not, Robert."

"Dr. Lewis. Do we think that this thing is airborne?"

"Madam Secretary, there is nothing in the data we have that would indicate that we are dealing with an airborne virus. If it were airborne, we'd have a lot more cases."

"What is the status of the patient in Boston?"

"He is still alive, but it's not looking good."

"Richard, have you gotten the results from the tests up in Maryland?"

"Not yet, sir. I'm waiting on them any minute."

"Please keep me appraised when you do get them," directed the National Security Advisor.

"We are going to need to get some information to the public," called Secretary Mitchell. "Richard, please take the lead on that and coordinate with my office when you have a draft," she continued.

"Yes, Madam Secretary."

"Unless anyone else has something to say, we need to conclude this meeting and get to work," called the cabinet member. The phone line was silent. "Then, that's it. Goodbye," concluded Jules Mitchell. Pausing for ten seconds after concluding the call, she pondered the potential outcome. Jules pressed down on a phone key to call her assistant.

"Bonnie, get me the President," she called into the speakerphone.

* * *

Dream Challenge

Tony sat in his hospital bed alone as he wrote two letters on separate pieces of paper. It was late in the evening and he knew that as soon as he fell asleep, he would enter the seventh dream challenge. The first letter was to Melissa.

Melissa,

I know that you will not understand, but if you are reading this letter, I am dead. The circumstances surrounding my death are not what the media will say it is. I cannot explain it, nor elaborate on it, but make me one promise. Do not accept the cause of death. Also, do not try and find out what really happened to me. Please go on and live your life and be happy. You are a remarkable woman. I love you dearly.

- Tony

He carefully stuffed the note into a small envelope, sealed it, and appropriately addressed it to his girlfriend. After a brief pause, he started on the second letter.

Alison,

If you are reading this note, then you made it out, but I did not. I am sorry, so very sorry. When I met you and started to have feelings for you, I questioned myself, as I was already in love with another woman. That love faded and my feelings for you only grew stronger. You are a beautiful woman and I only wish that I could have spent more time with you.

Regarding the dream challenges. Mr. Y killed me and likely many others. During one of my challenges, he explained the rules to me. There are seven challenge nights, in consecutive order. Any contestant that fails to complete one challenge in seven nights, dies in real life. I am sure you experienced the feeling in real life when you failed multiple dreams. I know I did. I was given an opportunity to bring a previously successful challenge contestant, back into the game. I chose you. I am sorry, but I had to see you again. Bringing you back was the only way I knew how. When you came back into the game, I was unable to explain the rules to you. I knew that if you beat Mr. Y once – you could do it again.

I truly wish that you didn't have to read this note and instead would be spending time with me in Boston. I failed on that wish, but ask that you do me a favor. Please work with the CDC in Atlanta, and figure out a way to kill that son-of-a-bitch Mr. Y. Dr. Richard Lewis is the man to see. Also, please know that I fell in love with you as I entered my last dream challenge. Please see Dr. Lewis and find a way to prevent *what happened to me, from happening to others. This is my last wish. I have faith in you.*

Love,

- Tony

Tony signed and sealed the second note and placed both letters on the table next to his bed. If he succeeded in the final dream challenge, he would wake up and destroy both letters. Tony took a deep breath and closed his eyes, sinking down into the bed as he readied for sleep.

"Time for battle," he whispered.

18 – RACING THE AMAZON

Tony, Alison, and Casey levitated in a space that was near pitch black.

"Where the hell are we?" called out Casey from the darkness. "Who else is here?" he continued.

"I'm here Casey," replied Tony. "Alison, are you here too?"

"Yes, I'm here. Unfortunately," she replied after a brief pause. From the sound of their voices, they appeared to be facing one another in the shape of a triangle. None of them could see anything beyond pure darkness. After the initial comments confirmed that they had all returned to another night's challenge, the only sound audible was the asynchronous sound of their breathing. Tony could, however, smell Alison's perfume. He breathed in deeply, trying to drink the flavor of the fragrance. The calm was interrupted by the sound of a light switch cord being pulled. Instantly, an eerie red light positioned over the contestants, illuminated their faces.

Mr. Y, now in the center of the group, slowly rotated in a circle so that each contestant could see his face. All Tony could see were dimly lit faces, and currently he was looking at the back of Mr. Y's gray covered head. He also couldn't feel the ground, let alone see it.

"Good evening, everybody. Did you sleep well last night?" joked Mr. Y.

"Shut up!" called out Casey, staring directly at the host. "You crooked toothed, gray bearded bastard. Who put you in charge anyway?" he continued. After a brief pause, the rant continued. "Hey man, I'm not digging this gig anymore and want out. Why do I keep showing up at these things each night?" he questioned. "This is my third one of these stupid *challenges*," he mocked. Tony an Alison didn't respond. Tony wanted to, but knew that he would jeopardize Alison's safety if he even hinted about the rules of engagement. Whatever kept bringing the three of them back into Mr. Y's strange and subconscious world was a mystery. No one in the group, other than Tony, had any knowledge or control. As Mr. Y rotated towards Tony, his face became visible under the red light. Winking at Tony, he started a series of questions.

"Ms. Watson. Tell me, what do you know about the jungle?"

"The jungle, why?" returned Alison with a quizzical expression on her face. As the host rotated towards Tony, he asked again.

"What about you, Mr. Blackwell. Do you know anything about the vast jungles and their inhabitants that occupy this great planet of ours?"

"Yeah, I know a bit," replied Tony.

"Like what? Entertain me," responded the host as he continued to rotate back towards Casey Wilson, still enraged by the fact that he has no control of his dreams or Mr. Y.

"Well, I know that there are many jungles in the world, spanning from southeast Asia in Thailand and Cambodia, to northern Africa, and obviously, the Amazon in South America," he continued as his knowledge amazed even the host.

"I'm impressed, Mr. Blackwell. The Amazon it is then. That's where our next challenge must be," he concluded. Mr. Y prepared to snap his fingers.

"No!" called out Casey, but it was too late. *Snap!*

Instantly, the three challengers were transported from the dark room to a treetop stand, high in the jungle. The stand was positioned one hundred feet in the air, and contained built-in benches for all three. Each contestant looked around at their environment, and eventually leaned over the railing to see the ground far below. There was no obvious way to get down to the ground. Casey turned to look at Alison, who with Tony, was leaning over the railing and looking at the ground below. After a long stare, he sat down on the bench and called to Alison.

"Hey sweetie, why don't you come over and sit next to me," called Casey, while putting his hand on the open bench next to him. There was only enough room on the bench for three, so if Alison wanted to sit, she would have to sit close to somebody.

"Come on Alison, you can sit next to me," replied Tony with a harsh glance towards Casey. She reached out for Tony's hand and walked towards the bench. As the pseudo-couple turned to sit down, Casey placed his hand on the bench, palm facing upwards. Within moments, Alison felt the uncomfortable palm of Casey Wilson on her backside, and instantly jumped.

"Hey! What are you doing?" she responded.

"Sorry, I forgot to move my hands," he playfully responded, with a perverted look in his eyes.

"I swear to God, I'm going to kill you!" stated Tony, as he sprang up from the bench and grabbed Casey by the throat. His hand-to-hand military combat training jumped to life. Unfortunately, Casey was too strong for Tony. He quickly removed the adversary's hands from his neck, spun him around, and jammed Tony's left arm up the center of his own back.

"Ah!" replied Tony as Casey drove his arm higher, inflicting major pain. In doing so, he pushed Tony towards the edge of the railing and forced his head down with his free hand.

"You want to die, man?" asked Casey, teeth gnashed together.

"That's enough, Mr. Wilson," commanded Mr. Y, hovering directly above the group. Casey looked straight up as he continued to apply pressure to Tony's arm. "I said that's enough!" With the snap of his fingers, Tony was released and collapsed to the floor of the tree stand. Casey was strapped to a tree hanging high above the ground, ropes restricting his arms and legs.

"Let me out of here!" demanded Casey, attempting to squirm out from the clasp of ropes to no avail.

"Not until you can calm down, Mr. Wilson," continued Mr. Y, now lowering himself to eye level even with each of the remaining contestants. "You've become quite an annoyance, Casey. Do you recognize that Mr. Wilson?"

"Shut up! I swear I'm going to kill you one of these days," continued Casey.

"Not likely," returned the host, clearly in control. "So, where was I? Ah, yes. Tonight we are going to have an obstacle race through the glorious Amazon jungle. It's one of the last pristine places on Earth that produces tremendous and much needed oxygen for the world. Did you know that Mr. Blackwell?" Tony just stared at Mr. Y and didn't respond. He got up from the floor and dusted himself off from the brief fight with Casey. Alison moved quickly towards Tony.

"Are you ok Tony? I thought he was going to break your arm."

"Yeah, I'm ok," he quietly muttered, still skulking from his loss.

"Well anyway, the Amazon is one of the richest places on the planet and boasts some of the most incredible biodiversity in the world," continued Mr. Y. "It also contains some of the most lethal animals and plants, so be careful on your quest," he warned.

"What quest?" asked Alison.

"Your quest *is* to race through the Amazon," responded Mr. Y, with a warm smile. "Let me explain. You will all have sixty seconds to navigate an obstacle course that winds its way through certain terrain and challenges in this large and expansive place. I have taken the liberty of designing my own course. I'm actually quite proud of it," continued the host. "The course will challenge and entertain you. And it starts right here," he concluded, pointing to the cable line and handle above their heads.

"Is that a towline?" asked Alison.

"Sure looks like one," replied Tony as he stood up on the bench for a closer look at the equipment. He then gazed down the line to see where it went. "Where does it go?"

"That, Mr. Blackwell, you will have to find out for yourself," replied Mr. Y. "Now, let's get going, shall we? Alison, you will be the first contestant tonight, followed by Mr. Blackwell. Mr. Wilson will go last, right tough guy?" taunted Mr. Y, looking directly at Casey, who was still tied to the tree.

"I *will* kill you, you son-of-a-bitch," called out Casey.

"Ms. Watson. Are you ready, my dear?" After the question was asked, the tow rope handle automatically released and slotted into place directly above a small platform connected to the loft. A small swinging door connected the tree stand to the towline platform.

Alison unlatched the gate and passed through to the smaller platform, reached up, and grabbed the towline's handle.

"Alison!" called out Tony.

"Yeah?" she returned, looking over her shoulder at him as Tony approached the gate. Tony leaned in and gave her a kiss on the cheek.

"Good luck," he whispered. "Oh yeah, Boston," he continued.

"Boston? What does that mean?"

"I live in Boston," he returned with a warm smile, remembering that she lived in

Seattle. "I'll find you when we both win tonight. See you on the other side," he concluded, and blew her a kiss.

"Ok, love birds. Ms. Watson. When you pull down on the handle, it will release. Good luck," stated Mr. Y as he raised his trusty stopwatch and reset the timer. "Remember, sixty seconds." Alison nodded with understanding. She took a few deep breaths and waited for Mr. Y.

"Three, two, one, go!" shouted the host.

Alison grabbed the handle with both hands and jumped off the high platform, trusting that it would hold her. The latch released as promised, and she started to rapidly descend along the treetop zip line. As she gained speed rapidly, she began to wonder what was on the other side of the zip line. Tree leaves slashed against her arms and legs as she increased speed. After a ten second ride, the line flattened out and decreased the rate of speed. Within moments, Alison could see another mid-level treetop-landing zone. She instinctively pulled her legs up and prepared to land on the target wooden platform. Once securely on the deck, she yelled back to Tony "I'm ok!"

On the other side of the platform, which stood at approximately fifty feet off the ground, Alison spotted another towline. She raced across the ten-foot platform and grabbed the second handle. The second towline took Alison down again. Slicing through the air at twenty miles an hour, she could see the ground approaching. As she neared the ground, the towline dipped again, causing her rate to diminish greatly. Like a finely tuned athlete, Alison hit the ground running as the towline and land converged.

Red stakes on either side of a worn path guided her direction. Her heart raced. She ran as fast as she could through the winding course. Tree limbs with thick foliage often got in her way, causing her to duck and even crawl to continue on the path ahead. *Thirty seconds.*

Fists clenched and now sweating, she pressed on. A large animal's roar was heard in the near distance, but she didn't stop running. Alison's eyes darted left and right, looking for signs of trouble. *All clear.*

"Run goddammit!" she huffed aloud. Up ahead was a small stream that crossed her path. She kept pace as she approached it and leapt over the five-foot swath of water. In midair, a waiting crocodile snapped at her heels, just missing as she soared through the air.

"Holy shit!" exhaled Alison as she looked back at the reptile, still running. The trail narrowed and turned slightly left. As she punched through a dense ground cover of leaves, a series of wires ahead forced her to stop and drop to her knees. The wires extended horizontally across the trail at about three feet high and lasted for five feet in length. Alison moved as fast as she could, crawling on all fours below the wires. The red dirt covered her hands and knees as she continued through the obstacle course. As she neared the end of the wired tunnel, she stood up, but grazed the last wire as she rose. The wired trap delivered a powerful electrical shock to Alison, causing her to fall to the ground.

"Oh my God!" she cried. The jolt had affected her nervous system. "Keep going!" she yelled. Slowly, Alison regained her balance and stood up. The red flags directed a path to the right. She followed with a somewhat reduced pace. Within ten feet, the grass and trees surrounding the path, was replaced with tall bamboo-lined trees on either side. Some fifty feet ahead, Alison saw the finish line. Her heart pounded and her whole body ached from the electrical shock. As she made the final push towards the line, she caught movement out of the corner of her eyes on both sides of the bamboo trees.

Something is following me. Two shadows moved in tandem with her on either side of the trees. Strategically positioned indigenous Amazon pigmy warriors held positions up ahead near the finish line. Alison ran with all her might. As she approached the end of the course, the pigmy warriors raised small wooden pipes to their mouths. *Faster, faster,* thought Alison as she used all of her strength to keep running through the bamboo gauntlet. *Ten more feet.* As she approached the finish line, she stumbled and fell to the ground.

Moments before, the Amazon warriors had launched an array of poison darts at Alison, but missed! As the pigmy's reloaded their weapons with the deadly toxin, Alison scrambled to her feet and lunged towards the finish line, crossing it in midair and landing on the ground, stomach first. Exhausted, but alive, Alison had made it to the end of the challenging course.

"Fifty-nine seconds, Ms. Watson. Very nice, but close," stated Mr. Y, who now hovered just a few feet past the finish line. Alison smiled and closed her eyes. *It was all over.*

"Mr. Blackwell, I have good news," stated Mr. Y, who moments before had reappeared to the remaining participants. "Your friend, Ms. Watson, passed her latest challenge. She's free," mocked Mr. Y.

Tony smiled and instead of showing anger towards the host, he thought of a time when he and Alison would be reunited in the real world.

"Now for the bad news," stated the host as he turned and put his back towards Casey Wilson. "If you fail this challenge, your seventh in as many nights, you will *die in real life*," stated Mr. Y, whispering the last four words slowly. Tony just glared at him, opting to keep his thoughts and words to himself. "Nice try, Tony. I can read your mind too," continued the magical host. Mr. Y floated away and towards Casey Wilson. *Snap!*

The ropes that bound Casey to the tree snapped, causing him to free fall, yelling all the way down until he hit the ground below.

The delayed thud made its way to the tree stand a hundred feet up about a half second later. Tony looked over the railing in amazement, mouth wide open, then turned towards Mr. Y to speak. As he reached for something to say, nothing came out.

"Cat got your tongue, Mr. Blackwell? I never liked that guy anyway," continued Mr. Y. "Nobody really likes a true asshole and who in the hell names their son *Casey* anyway? If I didn't kill him, he would have hurt somebody else, maybe even you. That's just not in the rules." Tony continued to stare at the strange host, speechless. After an awkward pause, Tony moved towards the starting location of the towline, passed through the gate, and reached up to securely take hold of the dangling bar.

"I'm ready," he said, taking charge of the situation.

"Wow, very impressive Mr. Blackwell. You know. I actually hope that you do complete the challenge in less than sixty seconds. I think you deserve it. You have worked harder than most of my contestants and never gave up. Best of luck Tony."

"Why are we here?"questioned Blackwell.

"Excuse me, Tony?"

"You heard me. Why are we here?" repeated Tony with no expression on his face.

"Because, I selected you," returned Mr. Y. "That's all you get to know for now," he concluded, as he raised his stopwatch to eye level. Once the timer was cleared of the prior time, the two stared at each other for what seemed like an eternity. "Ready, set," started Mr. Y. Tony tightened his grip on the bar above his head, and then turned away from his intense stare at Mr. Y. "Go!" shouted the host as he started the clock.

Tony jumped off the platform and raised his legs up in a crouched position to ensure maximum speed. As he sped along the zip line, he tried to keep count of the precious seconds he consumed. This challenge was his last chance to succeed and he needed to pass. Branches and leaves slapped up against him as his speed increased. Seven seconds later, the rate of speed decreased as he neared the second treetop platform. With an athletic skill, Tony transitioned to the open wooden platform with one foot and ran across it to the other side. *Fifteen seconds.*

Tony jumped off the platform and grabbed the second handle, again bringing his feet up to his chest to increase speed. Slicing through the moist and stagnant jungle air, he continued counting. As the ground approached and the line drew slack, he hit the ground running. Like an NFL running back, he paused for nothing and intensely focused on the task at hand. His heart pumped. Determined as ever, Tony transitioned to a run and followed the red stakes that were laid out on either side of the dark red dirt path.

"You've got this Blackwell," he said, gritting his teeth together as he ran. As he neared a stream that crossed his path, Tony slowed his pace to take in the surroundings. "Son-of-a-bitch! A crock?" he gasped, as he spotted the creature wading in the water on the other side of the bank, just waiting for prey to cross. "Not this time," huffed Tony, as he diverted from the path and raced into the woods at a thirty-degree angle to the reptile, still moving towards the stream, but behind the beast.

Dream Challenge

Knowing that it would take the crocodile longer to turn around than jut forward, he sprinted. Ducking branches and weaving in and out of small trees, Tony continued until he reached the stream, away from the waiting crocodile. Slowing briefly, he jumped over the water and landed safely on the other side, only to be met by the hiss of a large boa constrictor hanging from one of the larger tree branches. Tony pushed it aside with his arm, and continued to run, eventually rejoining the red-staked path. *Thirty seconds.*

After expertly maneuvering through the wire trap, Tony stood and ran as fast as he could through the winding jungle course, constantly scanning the sides for trouble. *Nothing. Forty-five seconds.*

As he rounded a corner, he noticed a troupe of monkeys chanting and swinging from tree to tree. Some of the primates jumped up and down on the branches and screeched in unison. *Are they rooting for me?* he thought, then smiled. Tony pressed on and continued to sprint to the finish line ahead.

"There it is!" called out Tony, clearly seeing and pointing to the finish line ahead.

"I'm going to make it," he stated, sweat pouring down his face as he gasped for air. *Twenty more feet, and I've made it,* thought Tony. Tony allowed himself a small smile as he jogged towards the finish line. Images of Alison appeared in his head. He knew that he would find her in Seattle and that they would be together soon.

Thump, thump! Stunned, Tony stopped dead in his tracks, merely feet before the end of the obstacle course. As he looked at the finish line, his vision blurred and the muscles in his body went partially limp. Dropping to one knee, Tony reached up to his neck. He felt two small darts firmly entrenched under the skin and subsequently yanked one of the lances out of his neck and cried out. "Help me, please!" The words fell on deaf ears as there was no one in the jungle that would help him.

Still struggling on the ground, Tony crawled towards the finish line. He still counted the seconds in his head as the clocked ticked towards sixty. He crossed over the white finish line and fell onto his back, completely exhausted. *I made it!* he screamed to himself in exhausted silence. He had completed the seventh dream challenge. Trying to fight the venom gushing through his veins, Tony blinked both eyes rapidly in an attempt to regain clarity of his vision. Tears welled up in his eyes and prevented him from seeing clearly.

The jungle treetops spun above him and his vision worsened with the moisture and stress. The pain set in over his entire body. Tony's fingers and arms began to atrophy, causing near full loss of mobility in much of his extremities. "No!" he called out, eyes blinking rapidly in succession as sweat and tears rolled down his cheeks. He was rapidly losing the battle against the dangerous toxin. His eyelids became heavy.

Tony attempted to widen his eyes to stay cognizant. As he did so, the image of a jungle warrior, complete with black and yellow war paint, came into view. The tribal aggressor stood directly over Tony and stared down at him with curiosity. Within moments, additional warriors pushed through the foliage and flanked the lead shooter. Each member of the hunting party exhibited their own unique war paint, artfully displayed across their chest, arms and face. The team of indigenous fighters stood silently above their prey in a circle. Tony opened his mouth and tried to speak. His eyes fluttered as his body violently fought against the venom. Convulsions began to set in. The struggle was useless and eventually he lost the battle with the conscious world as his eyes fell shut. *Snap!*

19 – PROJECT ADOBE-322

Goddammit, resuscitate him Dr. Boxer!" shouted Dr. Smith. "Phil?" he called out again, this time with a more personal appeal, clearly not satisfied with the original response. The tone from the heart monitor was constant and flat.

"Clear," responded Dr. Boxer. He charged, shocked, and pumped the patient for another thirty seconds. Sweat poured down his face. Phil was clearly exhausted and frustrated. As the resuscitation attempt came to an end, it appeared the team had lost yet another patient. Suddenly, the familiar sound of a heartbeat filled the room. The pulsing started out slow and weak, but gained in strength quickly as it reached nearly sixty beats a minute.

"Yes!" exclaimed Dr. Smith. "The patient is going to make it," he exulted. The team worked for the better part of thirty minutes to stabilize Tony. As they did, he stayed lifeless on the table, but alive. After further inspection by the elite medical team, it was determined that Tony had slipped into a coma.

Dr. Richard Lewis watched from the raised observation room without emotion and retrieved his Boeing Black smart phone from his hip cradle. His entire team traveled with specially made smart phones that were capable of sending NSA-level encrypted messages designed to prevent prying eyes and potentially worse, press leaks.

Secure Message Alert: *Project Adobe-322*

Mr. Blackwell survived, but is in a coma.

Dream Challenge

Call an emergency meeting with the WHO and notify the Director of the CDC, plus the National Security Advisor at the White House. This is now a matter of national security.

We need to interview the patient when he comes out of the coma, but we have no idea when that will be – if ever.

- Dr. Richard Lewis

Tony Blackwell lay face up on the table, his eyes calmly closed. Although his body was heavily bruised, there appeared a certain peaceful demeanor to those observing. He lay stone still. The team transported him to the intensive care section of the hospital, where a team would monitor his vitals around the clock.

* * *

Alison woke from her dream in the confines of her apartment. Her bed sheet and cover crisscrossed the floor as if they had been violently ripped off the bed via a struggle with an intruder. Her heart raced. She glanced at the clock. It was 3:00 a.m. Pacific time, and still dark outside. As she rose from her bed, she allowed a small smile to grace her face. She had beaten Mr. Y

271

during the most recent and amazing Amazon obstacle course.

"What a rush that was," she stated, as she walked to the kitchen for a drink of orange juice. As she gulped down the chilled citrus, her mind wandered off the very recent challenge to Tony. Placing the near-empty glass on the counter, she moved to the family room and opened her laptop. As it booted, she wiped the sweat from her face. Wet hair dangled in front of her face as if she had just gotten out of a hot shower. Within moments, she was online and using her favorite search engine.

Keyword Search: *"Tony Blackwell"*

Results / Pages: *29,204 links*

Alison revised the search to include *Tony Blackwell +Boston*, then hit the enter key. Ninety-eight results appeared. Satisfied with her efforts, she crossed her legs and settled in for a late night of research. She remembered that Tony was from Boston and that he would potentially try to find her after they both completed their challenge. *Did he win?* Following the next link, a LinkedIn profile page appeared with limited information about a Tony Blackwell found on the site. *Is this the right Tony?* Following instructions on the LinkedIn web site, she created her own profile, uploaded a picture of herself, and then attempted to make contact with the individual named Tony that she had found. Playing it safe, she typed a message that only Tony would know.

Message: *Do you know Mr. Y? –Alison.*

She would have to wait a bit to know for sure. Continuing on, Alison worked her way through the list of ninety-eight search results. Then it happened. She stumbled onto a Facebook profile page with a picture of *her* Tony. Although most of the profile page was private, there were a few pictures posted and limited text for the public to view, one of which contained a picture of a pretty Brunette with her arm around Tony Blackwell, simply titled *Melissa*.

"Who in the hell is Melissa?" huffed Alison, with a hint of jealousy in her voice. After quickly logging into her Facebook account, she sent a message to Tony.

Message: *Tony - did you beat Mr. Y? I really hope so. Please call me at 206-870-1441 or reach me on Facebook. I miss you. Can't wait to see you. Standing by.*

– Alison.

Alison spent the next two hours researching Melissa on the same social networking site. She searched for any additional data about the woman pictured with Tony. The beeping sound of a new message startled Alison.

Message: *Sorry, I don't know Mr. Y, but do you want to meet Mr. XXX?*

"Oh, grow up," grunted Alison. "I'm getting rid of this freak right now," she continued as she typed her reply.

Message: *Sorry, wrong answer and wrong guy. Not interested.*

An hour later and nearly daybreak, Alison found a profile page of the woman that appeared on Tony's page. This profile page, unlike Tony's page, had much more information that was accessible to the public. She read the highlights aloud.

Melissa Stewart

Age: Twenty-six years old.

Status: Single, but in a serious relationship.

Education: B.A., Tufts University.

Dream Challenge

Profession: Teacher, Park Street Elementary School in Boston Massachusetts.

The woman depicted in the pictures was definitely pretty. Many of the photos that included Tony showed what appeared to be a happy couple. Two of the photos were dated in the current month.

"Shit. That is pretty damn recent," she stated. "I wonder why Tony never mentioned this girl to me. I guess all guys really *are* jerks," she continued with her one-way conversation. Frustrated, Alison closed the laptop and moved from her computer. The sun was coming up soon and she needed to get to work. Since Alison had only just recently re-entered the dream challenge and won, she wasn't bruised or sick in any manner. With mixed emotions running through her head, she attempted to block out the upsetting information about Tony's girlfriend by turning on the television. Turning the channel to a national news program, she tried to dig out of the emotional tunnel she was in. "Time to move on Alison" she forcefully stated, as she turned up the television volume and headed towards the shower.

* * *

The phone call pierced the silence of the small, cramped and sterile office. After three rings, the decorated officer answered. "Colonel Jones here."

"Reggie, its Richard Lewis."

"Dr. Lewis. What do I owe the pleasure of this call?"

"I need to talk to you about project Adobe-322."

"Not on *this* line you don't," shot back the officer, with a clear change in tone. Call me back on my STU," commanded Colonel Jones, referring to the standard issue military encrypted phone. Cipher keys were rotated daily to ensure the safety and security of conversations.

"I am not near a STU," responded the physician. I'm in my car near Massachusetts General Hospital."

"Then get near one, doctor! You know how to reach me. Good day," concluded Reggie Jones, who promptly hung up the phone. *The nerve of that guy.* "What the hell was he thinking uttering a Top Secret compartmented phrase on an unsecured line? Shit." Clearly perplexed by the spontaneous call, the soldier leaned back in his chair and postulated the reason for the call and more importantly, the sensitive topic.

Reggie opened the cedar humidor in front of him, lit a cigar, turned towards his secure computer, and typed the phrase *Black Operations+Adobe-322*. Colonel Jones paused briefly before hitting the enter key. The grizzled Army officer and decorated Ranger knew what he was about to do, but did so anyway. Every Top Secret computer search was logged, creating an audit trail to ensure the nation's most secret content stayed hidden.

The security gurus at the NSA frequently analyzed classified search requests, results, and research patterns via programmed search botnets. Botnet code was efficient and designed to look for connections across multiple sources and for links between different individuals running related searches at various dates and times.

Reggie systematically reviewed several documents from a U.S. cold war project sponsored by the CIA that appeared to be related to project Adobe-322. Few in the Army even had such computer access privileges. Colonel Jones also knew that when anyone searched folders that contained highly classified information, it triggered an alert to several key resources in the Pentagon and the NSA. Reggie pressed on and read about the Top Secret program as he waited for his colleague and friend to call him back on a secure line.

* * *

Using his secure Boeing Black phone, Dr. Richard Lewis searched for and found the closest military installation from his current location. *Four miles.* He typed the address into the GPS system and within ten minutes, Dr. Lewis showed up at the front gate of the military installation.

"May I help you, sir?" asked the MP guarding the gate. Dr. Lewis sat in his comfortable civilian car without any government or military markings.

"Yes, you may," replied Richard Lewis, flashing his badge and handing the man an envelope that contained an authorized letter from the head of the CDC. The sergeant reviewed the letter and looked closely at the CDC badge presented by Dr. Lewis.

"What can I do for you, sir?"

"I need to use a secure phone immediately," he demanded. The Marine promptly walked to the security station and placed a call. Within moments, he returned to the side of the car.

"Dr. Lewis. Please drive fifty yards, turn left, and then park outside building 3R. Someone will meet you there." Lewis simply nodded, rolled up the window, and waited for the Marine to raise the gate. Upon doing so, he moved the car forward and accelerated. Time was of the essence and he needed to find out if the secret black operations program was still active. As Richard stopped the car outside of building 3R, a young Marine captain met him in the parking lot.

"Come with me Dr. Lewis," said his escort as he led the CDC professional to a conference room equipped with secure phones. "I am Captain…"

"Save it soldier," cut off the impatient doctor. "Just take me to the office with the STU."

"Yes, sir." When they arrived, the Captain left the private office as fast as he had escorted the guest there. "Take your time, sir. I will make sure that you are not interrupted. Do you have the number of the person you are calling?"

"Yes." It was committed to memory.

"Excellent. I will be right outside if you need anything."

"Thank you Captain." Richard Lewis settled into the chair opposite a bank of secure phones. He selected one, picked up the receiver and dialed. Four rings later, Colonel Jones answered from his office in Frederick, Maryland.

"Colonel Jones. Is that you, Richard?"

"Yes, Reggie." The sound on the STU was all too familiar. The voices were clear, but echoed a bit and reminded Dr. Lewis of what a conversation with Donald Duck would be like.

"What is this all about Richard?"

"I need to know if the highly compartmented Adobe-322 is still active," stated Dr. Lewis.

"Boy, you sure do cut to the chase when you want something," responded Colonel Jones. "No. It is *not* active. The Adobe-322 program was shut down in 2010 after we appeared to be on solid ground with the Russians. I wish we still had it today, though," he continued. "The current situation with North Korea is getting out of control and going in the wrong direction. We could be headed for nuclear war soon," he continued. "If we had 322, we could use it to wipe out the North Korean elite and program it to kill a particular DNA strain."

"Jesus, Reggie. We have enough to worry about now as it is. Are you sure the program is no longer active – anywhere?"

"Oh yeah. I am looking at the project data right now. The report says that the CIA ceased testing in May of 2009 and that all subjects were disposed of in a manner fitting the project goals."

"Where are the remaining vials?"

"Right here at Fort Detrick, twenty of them."

"Is there any chance a portion of the virus could have been stolen?"

"Highly unlikely, Richard. We keep the Biosafety Level 4 Lab (BSL-4) agents tightly controlled and locked up tight. The pathogens inside our BSL-4 lab include Marburg, Ebola, Lassa, the Congo hemorrhagic fever, and of course, our man-made weapons like Adobe-322. What's this all about Richard?" asked the Army specialist.

"Over the last few months, the CDC received a fair number of reports from hospitals around the globe, where patients died from a rapidly progressing illness that resembled Ebola-like symptoms. To date, there are no known survivors, except for one young man in Boston. He's currently in a coma at Massachusetts General Hospital. Any patients who died that *were* tested against our standard list of pathogens, including Ebola, have come up negative. We have obviously *not* tested any of the deceased against Adobe-322," stated Dr. Lewis. Reggie Jones paused and acknowledged the information.

"Reggie. What about the scientist who stole Anthrax a couple of years ago and sent envelopes to a few folks at the United States Congress? Did he have access to everything in the BSL-4?"

"Unfortunately, yes," replied the officer, now less confident than before.

"So, it is possible that someone might have taken a small amount? Goddammit Reggie. Which is it, *yes* or *no*?" After a longer than normal pause, the officer answered.

"It is possible. But very unlikely."

"Shit! I am going to have to get back to you on this my friend. Let me know if you find out anything else about this program that was supposedly shut down."

"Richard, I take it I am going to get some inquiries on this one. Is that true?"

"Highly likely. Keep me informed Colonel. That is an order."

"Sure thing," replied Colonel Jones as he prepared to hang up the secure phone. "And by the way, Richard. I do *not* work for you, so don't order me around like some private," he growled before taking a long drag on the Cuban cigar still burning bright with reddish-orange embers. The phone line went dead.

Dr. Lewis sat alone in the secure conference room and contemplated the information he had just been given by his trusted military friend. The physician turned to his smart phone and entered a secure message.

<u>*Secure Message Alert*</u>:

Alice – please book me a call with the NSA in DC. Subject of the call: Project Adobe-322. Classified: Top Secret, Compartment 55/322.

- Dr. Richard Lewis

20 – INTRODUCTIONS

Melissa woke the next day at 10:00 a.m., alone in her apartment. She was not feeling well, so she decided to stay home from work for one more day. Another day of nausea and mild cramps caused her to stay tucked in bed. *Must be my period,* she thought. As she stared up at the ceiling while still under the covers, all Melissa could do was think about Tony and his complex physical and mental state. The doctors were doing everything they could to better understand Tony's rapidly progressing illness.

She closed her eyes and took a deep breath before rolling out of bed and walking to the television. As she turned on the news, Dr. Richard Lewis was speaking at a press event from the CDC's headquarters in Atlanta, Georgia.

"Are we looking at a viral epidemic Dr. Lewis?" questioned a member of the press. Twenty microphones and personal recorders sprang towards the podium as if they were threatening the speaker at a criminal deposition. Other reporters nearby simply watched and waited for the CDC expert to give his response.

"No, we do not have an epidemic at this time. I don't want to turn this press event into an emergency session or announce anything like an epidemic. Rather, my goal is to reassure the public that the CDC, working with various health organizations across the globe, is monitoring the situation and will advise the public on any risks and travel restrictions deemed necessary. For now, if you or anyone you know have the symptoms, please call your local hospital or the CDC directly via the hotline number listed on the screen below. Thank you. That is all I have today."

Dream Challenge

The symptoms, along with the CDC hotline phone number, scrolled across the screen's footer below the live image of the press conference. Dr. Richard Lewis looked composed, but clearly concerned. Melissa watched as the list of symptoms scrolled across the television. They were undeniably familiar. Muscle aches and pain throughout the body, bruising, and stiff extremities accelerated in body joints after three to four days of exposure. Internal bleeding occurred on day five and six, with death following on day seven. Melissa could only stare at the information plastered across the screen as if it were screaming at her.

"Oh my God!" Abruptly, Melissa sprinted to the bathroom and promptly threw up the contents of her stomach. With her head buried in the porcelain bowl and face flushed with blood, she tightly gripped the side of the toilet with both hands as her stomach tightened again. She slowly pulled away from the toilet after the horrid feeling subsided. Moving to the sink, she rinsed her face with cold water and regained control of her irregular breathing. Melissa slowly moved back to the family room to re-engage with the television. In shock and still listening, she reached for the phone and dialed.

"Mom. Are you looking at the news right now?"

"No, honey. Why, what is wrong?" responded, her mother, sensing her anxiety.

"Turn on CNN."

"What's the matter Melissa?" shot back her mother. "Are you alright?"

"Just do it!" shouted Melissa into the phone.

"Hold on a moment," her mother returned, as she searched for the remote control. "Got it." The next twenty seconds were silent on both sides of the call. "What does this mean honey?"

"Mom. These are the symptoms that Tony has," she softly stated, eyes still locked onto the television and void of any blinking or movement.

"Oh my gosh," responded her mother. "Let me go and get your father. Don't do anything. I will call you right back Melissa," she continued.

"Mom. I have *got* to call the CDC!" shouted Melissa. "Mom!"

The voice on the other end of the line went dead. Melissa pressed the call button and got a dial tone. Looking at the television, she called the CDC hotline and impatiently waited for three rings before a live person answered.

"You have reached the Centers for Disease Control and Prevention hotline. What is the nature of your call?" asked the friendly voice.

"I think my boyfriend has the symptoms that are being reported all over the news right now," replied Melissa, her voice trembling.

"Calm down, ma'am, so we can take your complete information."

"He is really sick and it has been seven days since he first experienced symptoms," explained Melissa. "Also, the doctor says he is in a coma and may never come out of it!" shouted Melissa, as her heart raced and heaved inside her chest. Thoughts raced through her head as the charming woman on the phone walked her through a series of questions. *How many others are there with similar symptoms? Am I at risk? Why do I keep throwing up all the time?*

"One more question Ms. Stewart, and this one is important. Do you have any of the symptoms that we've discussed and are also listed on the CDC website?"

"No."

"Ok. Thank you. I think I have everything that I need at this stage. I'll take your information and share it with our internal medicine team task force. Someone from that team will be in touch with you shortly to discuss your case," she continued.

"Thank you," whispered Melissa, finally getting control of her breathing as she tried to relax.

"Everything is going to be just fine young lady. We have the best minds in the world looking at this situation. Thank you for calling the CDC and try to have a nice day." Melissa didn't respond and the phone went dead again. *I have to call mom and dad back*, she thought as she gently placed the phone receiver back into the cradle.

* * *

A CDC physician, an older gentleman with a finely trimmed gray beard and bi-focal eyeglasses, sat motionless and gazed at the large screens embedded in the walls of the CDC *war room*. The screens projected a live running tally of patients associated with the new threat, along with their geographical location. As he watched, the tally ticked up by one as a new graphical pin was displayed in Boston, Massachusetts.

"That's *three* in the Northeast today," muttered the scientist, just loud enough for a colleague to turn his head and look up at the giant map.

Melissa sat in her apartment after the call with the CDC was finished and simply stared at the television. Flipping through the channels, she couldn't get away from the CDC alert. It was being discussed on every news channel. Standard network and cable channels ran breaking alert news banners at the bottom of the screen throughout the day to keep viewers updated on the public health situation.

Then it happened again. Melissa started to feel queasy and nauseous. She bolted for the bathroom and promptly threw up into the open sink.

* * *

Alison was on the mend, recovering at a rapid rate, after her recent win against Mr. Y. She watched the news from her living room regarding the CDC announcement in silence as she thumbed through the itinerary of her flight to the East coast.

"Shit, just go, Alison!" she interrupted the broadcast out loud. "You will never know if you don't just do it." Over the last two days, she researched even more about Tony's girlfriend. Cross checking Melissa's Facebook page with the white pages, she finally obtained her address in Boston. The process was surprisingly easy and aided by the large amount of public information that Melissa had exposed about herself on the Internet. Email address, work address, resident city, and instant message screen name were all accessible. Put them all together with a decent search engine and snap, finding a home address was easy.

Looking at her watch, Alison realized she had just two hours to get to the airport and make the next flight to Boston. With her bags packed and resting near the front door, she rocked back and forth with indecision in her eyes. Abruptly, Alison sprang up from the chair, strode towards the door, and grabbed her bags as she raced out of her apartment.

The cab ride to the Seattle-Tacoma International airport was quiet, too quiet. Retrieving her cell phone, she dialed her best friend.

"Rachel, it is me, Alison."

"What's up girl? How are you feeling today?"

"Fine. I'm going," she said bluntly.

"What?"

"You heard me. I have got to meet her."

"Does she know you're coming?"

"Of course not! How do you tee that meeting up? Hi, I met your boyfriend in a series of crazy dreams and fell in love with him?" she joked, while feeling nervous and perplexed.

"Do you want me to go with you?" her friend replied.

"No, but thank you. I have to do this on my own."

"Wow. So, what are you going to say to her? How in the hell can you pull something like this off anyway?"

"I have not figured it out yet, but have the entire plane ride to think and plan my approach," responded Alison. "Listen, don't tell anyone about this, ok? I'm taking some time off from work until I can get this whole thing figured out," replied Alison.

"Ok. Call me when it is all over. I am here for you if you need me." The line went dead, but she now had the attention of the cab driver, who had repeatedly glanced in the mirror over the last sixty seconds or so.

"Do you mind?" she rebuffed the driver as she felt short on patience with no plan of attack. Alison closed her eyes and waited for the car ride to finish and a longer ride to start. United Airlines flight 133 was waiting at the airport and would have her in Boston by 6:00 p.m.

* * *

Melissa spoke with her parents and told them of the conversation with the CDC. Concerned about her illness, her mother volunteered to come and visit for a couple of days, but Melissa declined.

"Any chance that you are pregnant?" her mother asked cautiously.

"God no. That would be just horrible," shot back Melissa at the thought of raising Tony's children without him.

"You can always find out sweetie with a quick test kit from the pharmacy," joked her mother, trying to calm her nerves.

"Mom. *Stop it*. Really!" begged Melissa. "Listen, I will be just fine. I have to run now mom. I love you and will talk to you later," she continued. When the phone line went dead, Melissa paused and thought for a moment about the possibility of being pregnant.

Pregnant? Not possible, she mused. A smile slowly came to her face after she realized that if she *were* pregnant, she would have something wonderful from Tony in her life forever. Melissa turned the television off, grabbed her keys from the counter, and headed out of her apartment. Walking out of her complex, she turned right and walked the sunny sidewalk at a casual pace, but with purpose. Within minutes, she entered the local CVS pharmacy and headed straight for the fertility isle.

"I cannot believe I am doing this," she quipped to herself, browsing through the different pregnancy test brands and packages. The internal joking didn't stop her from buying the test. After paying for the product, Melissa quickly stuffed it into her purse so that nobody else could see what she bought. She promptly left the store and headed home.

Back at her apartment, Melissa removed the pregnancy test and just stared at it. Moments passed, but the time was not right. She tossed the unopened package onto the table and went to the other room, where she could not see the test product. *Out of sight, out of mind.* The rest of the afternoon, Melissa kept herself busy by doing laundry and light classroom work in support of her teaching job. *Keep busy,* she silently told herself more than once, to avoid taking the test. It seemed to be working.

* * *

As the plane touched down at Logan International Airport in Boston, the brief jolt woke Alison from her catnap. Surprised that she had fallen asleep, she looked out the small window to see the Boston cityscape in the distance. It was beautiful and different from the west coast. As Alison admired the city from afar, a sense of uneasiness came across her, as she knew that her meeting with Melissa was drawing close.

"Welcome to Boston, ladies and gentleman," called out the captain. "We appreciate your business and know that you have a choice when flying these days. Thank you for flying United Airlines," continued the captain as he began to taxi the aircraft towards gate B5. As the plane neared the gate, Alison thought about her approach and made up her mind. Just take a taxi to the apartment, walk up, and introduce yourself.

"Hi, I am Alison. I know Tony in another life," she practiced. "That is just stupid," she said, mocking herself. "Get a hold of yourself Al. Just tell her the truth." After departing the plane with her small carry-on bag, she hailed a taxi.

"315 Beacon Street please," she directed the cabbie.

"Sure thing, young lady. Are you here for business or pleasure?"

"Neither," responded Alison bluntly. The conversation was now officially over. As the taxi sped through the winding tunnels below the Northeastern financial center, Alison just stared out the window at the blur of tiles inside the tunnel racing past her and imagined what she would say to Melissa. Frustrated at the prospect that there might not be a good ending to her trip, she closed her eyes and simply waited until the taxi arrived at its destination.

* * *

As Melissa walked through the family room, her eyes strayed towards the pregnancy test.

"Shit," she huffed, grabbed it off the table, and ripped the package open. "Let's put an end to the suspense once and for all," she grunted, as she walked towards the bathroom. Melissa slammed the door closed and began to douse the test device with her own urine. Sixty seconds later, she emerged from the bathroom with the device in hand. "We shall see in three minutes," she mused calmly and put the plastic thermometer-like device on the table again. Impatiently waiting for the results, Melissa turned on the television and began surfing channels that were not talking about the CDC warning.

* * *

Twenty-two minutes later, Alison arrived in front of the quaint apartment complex. "Here we are, ma'am."

"Thanks," replied Alison as she paid in cash. As the car sped off, Alison glanced at her watch. It was 6:45 p.m. and dinner time for most in the professional world. The sun was trying to crawl into its nightly hole and cast an eerie orange glow across the sky. "Here we go," stated Alison as she walked up the building steps. As she arrived at apartment 202, she stopped at the door and paused. Alison placed her bag on the floor and took a deep breath. *What the hell do I say to this woman?* Realizing that her bag was visible to the occupant of the apartment, she pushed it aside so that it was further away and didn't give the appearance that Alison was coming to stay for a while. Exhaling slowly, Alison knocked on the door three times, then took a step backwards.

Inside the apartment, Melissa gazed at the pregnancy test on the table. The green plus sign was clearly visible. With her mouth wide open in amazement, she started to call her mother, but paused at the knock on the front door. Stunned by the interruption, Melissa walked to the door and looked through the security hole to see a young woman on the other side of the door. Tilting her head ever so slightly to the side, she paused, and then opened the door.

"Can I help you?" asked Melissa, confused by the beautiful woman at her front door.

"Are you Melissa Stewart?"

"Yes."

"May I come in? I know Tony Blackwell," replied the attractive young woman. Melissa stood in shock looking at the woman, now taking in her natural beauty from top to bottom. Thoughts raced through her head in random order. *I have never seen this woman before in my life. Who the hell is she? How does she know my Tony? Oh my gosh – I'm pregnant!*

"I'm sorry. What did you say?"

"My name is Alison Watson. I know Tony. We need to talk. May I please come in?" she pleaded, a genuine expression on her face.

Melissa did not respond and simply opened the door while she searched for the right words that never came out. The pair walked into the apartment, Melissa in front of Alison. The television newscast was talking about the CDC warning. Alison canvassed the room, looking at the young girlfriend, then at the television, then at the pregnancy test on the table. *Oh my Gosh, it is positive!* Alison maintained her calm and showed no emotion on the outside. Inside, she was screaming. Melissa noticed the beautiful intruder looking at the pregnancy test and promptly picked it up and put it in her pant pocket.

"Melissa, I know that Tony is in the hospital," calmly stated Alison, still searching for the right words.

"How do you know that? I think he may have contracted whatever is going around that is being talked about on the news," replied Melissa, glancing at the television to avoid direct eye contact with the young woman. *God, please tell me that Tony really doesn't know her.*

"Is he alright?"

"He's in a coma," replied Melissa, now looking directly at the blond stranger.

"Did Tony tell you about his dreams?"

"Some of them," replied Melissa, with a quizzical look on her face. *How in the hell does she know this?* "Why? How do you know about them? Who are you again and how do you know my Tony?"

"My name is Alison. Alison Watson," she replied with no emotion.

"Who are you, really?" asked Melissa, now crying.

"Listen Melissa. I didn't ask to be in this nightmare, but it just happened," replied Alison, still searching for the right words to explain the bizarre series of dreams and how she fell in love with Tony. "What you see on television isn't the truth," she stated as she motioned to the television set still broadcasting the CDC message. "The Centers for Disease Control and Prevention doesn't have a clue about what's really happening around the globe. They call it an epidemic, but it's not one. It's something else that I can't explain," continued Alison.

"What the hell are you talking about!" yelled Melissa. "Get out of my house!" she continued and pointed to the front door. "Now!"

"Wait, please listen to me Melissa. Just give me five minutes," pleaded Alison. Melissa wanted her gone, but knew that this woman might have answers to so many questions she had swirling in her head.

"You have three," curtly replied Melissa.

"Ok, ok. Thank you, Melissa. I was in the same strange dream challenges that Tony experienced and likely talked to you about. Did he tell you the details about his dreams and about a guy named Mr. Y?" asked Alison as she sat down on the nearby couch.

"Yes."

"I am really sorry that Tony is in a coma, but I think I know what put him there," she continued. Melissa sat down on the couch, put her face into her hands, bent forward, and rocked back and forth. *How can this be happening to me?*

Alison moved closer towards the woman and put her hand on her leg. "I am sorry. I know this is a lot to take in, but you need to listen and focus on what I am about to tell you," continued Alison. "I was in some of the same dream challenges that Tony was in. I passed a recent one, broke the

303

chain of repeating nightly challenges and survived," she continued. Melissa looked up from her curled posture, confused as ever.

"What did you just say?"

"I said that I *survived*," repeated Alison, accentuating the last word. "I beat Mr. Y and went right before Tony did. Obviously since he is still alive, he must have beaten Mr. Y too," continued Alison.

"But then why is Tony in a coma? He should be recovering by now." Alison proceeded to describe many of the same dream challenges that Tony had expressed to Melissa, including the symptoms associated with not passing a challenge. Melissa's mind raced back and forth between the dreams and her pregnancy.

"So why are you here? What does any of this have to do with me and Tony?" asked Melissa.

"I think I know how I can help Tony and stop this nightmare from happening to anyone else," continued Melissa. "I also think I know how to kill that son-of-a-bitch Mr. Y," she said softly as she stared intensely into Melissa's eyes.

21– THE SWEET SMELL OF DEATH

Bethesda, Maryland

Dr. Victor Zolin sat in his modest office at the National Institutes of Health in Bethesda, Maryland. He'd been the lead scientist on dream research for the better part of the last decade. Funding had almost dried up a few years back, but thanks to an angel and an anonymous donor, Victor had the funds he needed to continue his research.

The research, frowned upon by most other scientists at NIH, seemed impalpable and not consistent with traditional scientific studies and research methodologies. Dr. Zolin had published several of his findings on subconscious dream activity in the Journal of Medicine, often becoming a focal point for scrutiny in the scientific community in Washington DC and the country as a whole.

As Dr. Zolin analyzed his most recent experiment from last night, his secure cell phone interrupted the process and jolted him away from the task.

"Hello?"

"Victor, it's me Yuri," responded the head of the powerful Russian SVR.

"Good morning, sir, or should I say good evening on your time," responded Victor.

Yuri Soblevsky ignored the reference to the time change and continued with the purpose of his call. "We've concluded all of the experimental runs Victor. It's time to shut down the tank and wait for instructions regarding the next phase of our important project."

"What is the next phase, sir?"

"You will receive instructions when I am ready to give them to you," responded the SVR spymaster. "For now, just shut down the instrument and prepare to go live with project *Zaytsev*. We will pay tribute to the great Russian sniper of World War II, Vasily Zaytsev.

"Yuri. I will need more bandwidth to continue with the satellite uplink," informed Dr. Zolin.

"Do it," responded the head of the SVR. "But, do it *quietly*. We don't need anyone in the United States government looking over our shoulder at NIH, now do we?"

"I will make the preparations, sir. It will be ready a week from tomorrow. My scientific cover is already established in support of the justification to add more bandwidth to the uplink. I stand ready to support you and Mother Russia," concluded Victor.

"Spasibo. Dosvidaniya comrade Zolin."

The phone went dead. Victor glanced over his shoulder at the custom-designed sleep chamber. He had spent countless hours designing and testing the system. The float tank was ten feet long, three wide and four feet deep and contained a highly concentrated and dense salt solution made up of magnesium sulfate to increase buoyancy. This allowed Victor to float effortlessly at a body temperature of 35.5 degrees Celsius, or 95.9 degrees Fahrenheit. Several intricate cables and measurement instruments were connected to the tank, including a significant satellite uplink connection. The connection allowed the system to communicate with any number of ground-based transmitters, which were linked to specific transponders on the satellites resting quietly above the planet. Victor had convinced the NIH procurement staff to purchase and configure bandwidth and transponder access on Iridium satellites as a mechanism to communicate in real-time and share his work with other leading scientists around the globe.

* * *

After a short and sometimes abrupt conversation, Melissa asked Alison to leave her apartment. The combination of jealousy, confusion, and anger prompted the request to immediately leave the premises. Alison stood outside of the apartment complex and waited for a taxi as she contemplated the recent discussion with Melissa Stewart.

"Shit. That didn't go well Alison," she stated with contempt in her voice. Alison extended her left arm to hail a taxicab. "Brilliant, just brilliant," she continued, clearly disappointed with her approach and the result. A yellow taxi pulled around the corner and up to the curb.

"Where to?" asked the driver.

"Logan International, please." Alison got into the car and slumped into the back seat as she contemplated her next step. *What do I do back home in Seattle? Should I go to the hospital and see Tony?* As the taxi pulled out into traffic, Alison called out to the driver from the back seat. "Change of plans. Take me to Massachusetts General Hospital first please."

"Yes, ma'am," responded the driver. Given the confusing streets of Boston, the cabbie could go eight blocks out of his way or make a U-turn at the upcoming busy intersection. *U-turn it is*, he thought, pulling on the steering wheel hard left to bring the bright yellow chariot around a hundred and eighty degrees.

Smash! At the exact instant the taxi achieved a hundred and twenty-degrees of the turn, a large landscaping nursery truck crashed into the passenger side of the vehicle. Tires screeched and glass shattered everywhere. The taxi driver slumped over the steering wheel after the airbag failed to deploy. This type of mechanical failure was common in Boston, as many taxis in the city were part of an aging fleet that failed to meet recommended maintenance schedules.

Alison was pinned to the side of the car as twisted metal from the impact had reduced the space in the back seat from two people to less than a single person.

"Help me!" she called out. Her leg was bleeding profusely and most likely broken along with multiple ribs. A couple of bystanders immediately came to the aid of the accident victims.

"Call 911!" yelled a man who approached the car from the passenger side. "Are you ok miss?" he called through the shattered window. Scanning from back to front, he noticed that the driver wasn't moving. The man came around to the driver's window, reached through the open window, and checked for a pulse. Nothing.

The driver was dead. "Oh my God," he whispered. Shifting back to the passenger window, the young man looked down and noticed that gas was leaking from the tank onto the road. "Get back," he called to the others who had come to help. "Get back! There's a gas leak. Where are those ambulances?" he called out in a panic.

"Gas is leaking?" questioned Alison. "Get me out of here!" she screamed.

Sirens rang in the distance. The rescue volunteer looked at his watch. *How long would it take the emergency team to get to the accident in traffic?* The fluid leaking from the car was streaming faster now. "Get away from that car!" yelled another bystander, cell phone glued to her ear as she called for help. Alison slid to the other side of the seat and slowly opened the opposite passenger door.

The pain seared into Alison's chest and leg. Falling to the ground, she started to crawl as best as she could as the rescuer continued to warn bystanders to get away from the car. In between warning announcements, the young man looked down and noticed that his shoes were soaked with gasoline. His mind told him to get the hell out of there, now. He broke into a sprint and headed for the sidewalk thirty feet away from the intersection. As he leapt over the curb, a large explosion rang out. The taxicab jumped off the asphalt in response. Flames and smoke billowed up into the sky. What was left of the car bounced back down to Earth as gravity pulled the burning wreckage back to the asphalt.

"Oh my God!" called out the man who initially ran towards the accident victims. The emergency vehicles were getting close. Unfortunately, they were too late. The man sat on the nearest curb and hung his head low. He anticipated the time he would need to spend with the police and emergency staff. Both the cab driver and passenger were dead. The day was about to get a lot longer.

* * *

Four days had passed since Alison's car accident. Her body was flown back to the west coast shortly after the accident at the request of her parents. The funeral was set to take place the following Saturday at Yarington's Funeral Home on 16th Avenue in Seattle, Washington. Family and friends arrived in Seattle to mourn their friend and beloved family member.

Dream Challenge

Melissa in Boston and Rachel in Seattle, each found out about the death of Alison Watson via CNN reporting. The reporter covered the Boston accident and took it nationally as part of a two-part series that discussed how autonomous cars were going to make streets in the United States safe again by leveraging computer algorithms versus reckless human drivers. Alison Watson and the taxi driver became a statistic of human-related accidents.

Rachel took in a deep breath as she joined the family members in mourning the death of her friend. Family and friends took turns talking about Alison and her life. Tears of joy and sorrow filled the room as the ritual continued well into the night.

Melissa Stewart sent flowers to the funeral home where Alison Watson's life was to be celebrated and mourned. *Flowers.* She paused and reflected on the day her younger brother died and how so many red roses were laid on his coffin. Melissa now felt guilty sending the woman home after their meeting in person. She envisioned bunches of roses laid out on top of her coffin. *The sweet smell of death,* thought Melissa. *How cruel life can be.*

22– RECOVERY

Melissa sat next to Tony's bed reading a book while Tony lay still. The sound of Tony's pulse and the automated breathing apparatus were the only sounds audible in the room. From time to time, Melissa would look up from her book and stare at Tony. *What if he doesn't come out of the coma? How do I raise this child without a father?* Tears welled up in her eyes and began to stream down her face. At that moment, the nurse appeared.

"Are you alright, honey?

"Yes. I'm fine," explained Melissa. "I'm sorry, I just can't believe that Tony is still in a coma after two weeks," she continued as she wiped the tears from her face with her forearm.

"If he is as strong as I think he is, he'll come back to you," stated the nurse, with a warm smile on her face.

"Thank you. I hope you're right." The nurse checked Tony's vitals, recorded several numbers from the instruments keeping Tony alive, and jotted them down on her iPad. Medical records at Mass General were all recorded on high tech devices that securely integrated into the hospital's Electronic Health Records (HER) Cerner system.

"You hang in there," stated the nurse before she exited the room.

* * *

Rachel reviewed Alison's cell phone and wondered if it was right to call the woman that Alison had just visited in Boston. She wanted to learn more about Alison's trip to

Boston to meet Tony's girlfriend, Melissa Stewart.

"Shit," huffed Rachel. "Alison, give me a sign will you? Should I just let this go or follow it through?" called out Rachel to her dead friend. Moments later, Rachel punched in the phone number and dialed.

"Hello?"

"Hi, is this Melissa Stewart?

"Yes, who is this?"

"I'm a friend of Alison Watson. She came to see you a few weeks ago from Seattle. Do you remember her?" Panic set in for Melissa. *Of course I remember her. She's dead! What does she want with me?* Melissa stood up and walked out into the hallway to continue the conversation.

"I remember. What is this about?"

"I just thought you should know that Alison confided in me about her dreams and about Tony."

"Interesting. What does that have to do with me?" asked Melissa. "By the way, did you know that my boyfriend Tony is still in a coma as a result of those creepy dream challenges?"

"No, I didn't know and I'm sorry to hear that Tony isn't doing well. Alison spoke very highly about Tony."

At that moment, two nurses raced by Melissa and into Tony's room. Surprised and shocked, Melissa dropped the cell phone and raced after them.

"Excuse me miss! You need to leave this room immediately, please. Tony's doctor is on the way. The monitoring equipment just notified us of a significant change in Tony's condition," called out the head nurse.

"I am not going anywhere," responded Melissa as she pushed past one of the nurses and took up a position at the bottom of Tony's bed. Staring directly at Tony, she couldn't believe her own eyes. Tony started to move his arms and legs, slowly but surely.

"Miss!" commanded the head nurse. "Please leave." Melissa stood her ground, folded her arms across her chest, and did not move an inch. Tears welled up and fell from her eyes as she saw what she thought she would never see again.

Tony's eyes twitched and then opened. He fully blinked multiple times. He appeared confused, but alert as if he was having trouble focusing his vision. Melissa moved to the side of the bed and took Tony's hand in hers and waited. Slowly, Tony turned his head and looked into Melissa's eyes. After blinking several more times, he smiled and softly said "M."

"Thank you God," responded Melissa.

The End

PROLOGUE:
DREAM CHALLENGE
REVENGE

<u>Tehran, Iran</u>

President Bahadur Amiri picked up the receiver on his secure phone and paused before dialing the number of the head of the Russian SVR. Looking out his office window, he saw the hot wind blow sand that appeared to be dancing in swirls outside the window of his compound. A typical day in Iran. His mind paused at the sheer power of the role that he had ascended. The office was decorated with ornate art and sculptures from hundreds to a thousand years ago. The Shiite leader contemplated his reign of control as he held the receiver in his hand. The president had total authority over the Ministry of Intelligence and Security, commonly referred to most often as MOIS or VEVAK (Vezarat-e-Ettela'at va Amniat-e Keshvar). MOIS officers are also only recruited by Shiites, true believers of the doctrine velayat-e-faqih.

MOIS had several responsibilities, among them, including foreign operations and intelligence gathering similar to the CIA and Mossad. Much of the foreign power of the MOIS had shifted to the Iranian Revolutionary Guards (IRGC). The IRGC operates under the control of the Supreme Leader.

President Amiri's presidency was at risk. It was common knowledge in the country and abroad that he and the Supreme Leader did not see eye to eye. The Supreme Leader and his supporting clerics appeared to be winning the power struggle with Amiri over control of the country. It was a matter of time before Amiri would be ousted, likely publicly by the Supreme Leader – regardless of whether he was elected by the public in a rigged election. Amiri sat quietly with the phone handset in his grasp. He knew he needed to do something bold to regain control over the office of the presidency in order to overturn the current state of affairs with the clerics actually running the country. Amiri dialed the number from memory.

"Sasha here," answered the powerful head of the SVR who always spoke in code name on the phone, regardless of whether the line was secure or not.

"Yuri. How are you my old friend?" returned Amiri, assessing his authority over the Moscow spy.

"Bahadur, please. You know how I feel about the Americans and their ability to intercept phone calls."

"Relax Yuri. We *are* secure. I'm confident that our new technology and the fact that we randomize and rotate encryption keys throughout the conversation cannot be detected by the Americans," replied Amiri. "Where do we stand with the trials?"

"We have completed them with full success and are ready to move forward with project Zaytsev," stated the Russian. A long pause ensued on the other end of the conversation.

"That is excellent news," responded the President of Iran. "Excellent indeed. Now let's discuss the final item on our agenda – the fee."

"Ah yes, the fee," laughed the Russian. "We request five million dollars per dose. We supply the weapon and the most beautiful spies to compromise the targets. Once attached and delivered, Russia wants nothing to do with the actual work on the ground President Amiri," calmly stated spymaster Soblevsky. "And we'll even throw in the technology to track and manipulate for free."

"Yuri, I think we can agree on that number. Since the Americans agreed to give us one hundred and fifty billion dollars in exchange for us stopping our military nuclear efforts, we can afford to buy multiple small countries, let alone a hundred doses of your bio-weapon. In addition, our oil sales to the Americans and their nefarious

European friends are on the rise," he laughed.

"We've been exploring ways to shudder the United States for decades." The powerful head of the SVR laughed and coughed into the phone.

"It's so ironic that the Americans are actually funding their own demise," responded President Amiri after a long pause.

"Payment via the typical channels please. No wire transfers or audit trail – just *gold* delivered to my man in Mosul, Iraq. We'll get it back to Moscow just fine from there," stated Yuri.

"Done," responded President Amiri.

"Agreed. I will let the president know immediately. Our business is then complete. Best of luck on your endeavor. Once we've received payment, we will deliver the weapons to your courier of choice in Afghanistan. Our conversation is now done my friend. I have a couple of young *devotchkas* waiting for me in the parlor, so I must go," concluded the Russian spymaster before disconnecting the line.

President Amiri softly placed the phone back on the cradle and contemplated his next bold move. A slow smile creased his lips as he knew he was about to undertake a process that no other in history had attempted or even conceived. He removed a cigar from the humidor on his desk and lit it. Comfortable with the amber glow of the tobacco, he placed the last and final call for the day to the Minister of Intelligence and Security.

"Yes?" responded Jafar Azodi, the Shiite head of the MOIS and a former IRGC officer.

"We are a go," responded President Amiri without referencing his name, office or title. Silence on the other end of the call ensued for fifteen seconds.

"Good. I will prepare my agents," responded the powerful head of the Intelligence service before hanging up the phone.

Jafar Azodi swiveled his chair a full one hundred and eighty degrees to view the large wallboard behind him. The board contained the structure and pictures of the United States cabinet members as well as key members of the House of Representatives and the U.S. Senate. A smile crept onto his bearded face. Reaching into a desk drawer, Azodi withdrew a small throwing knife and placed it into the palm of his right hand. He rocked back and forth as he contemplated the board in front of him. Azodi scanned the clear faces of the ugly American government leaders.

Suddenly, the knife went airborne. The throw was swift, deliberate, and accurate – piercing the photograph of the Director of the Central Intelligence Agency, or commonly known as the DCI. Azodi's smile broadened as he continued rocking in the chair. His stare intensified at the wallboard, now scanning each photo individually.

"It is just a matter of time before we make history and place the Arab world back on top of its rightful position in the world. Islam will rule and control the West," he whispered. "And I will be the one to deliver the pain. The arrogant United States of America is well overdue for a change in the world order," Azodi continued.

Jafar continued to rock back and forth as he intensified his stare at the pictures. "Praise Allah, he calmly stated. "Praise Iran."

AUTHOR BIO

Early in his career, Mr. Smith worked on a variety of United States government *Black* programs that required a *Top Secret* clearance with several security compartments above TS. He's leveraged his near-decade of national security work to paint his most recent project - *Dream Challenge*.

Mr. Smith is the author of *Dream Challenge*, *CIO 2.0*, *Straight to the Top: CIO Leadership in a Mobile, Social, and Cloud-based World*, *How to Protect Your Children on the Internet: A Road Map for Parents and Teachers*, and *Straight to the Top: Becoming a World-Class CIO*. His books are sold all over the world and have been translated into multiple languages, most recently Mandarin and Portuguese.

He has published many articles over his career, including *Talking at the Top of the World* in CIO magazine, along with a variety of technology and business topics in eWeek, The Wall Street Journal,

Computer World, CIO, and Network World magazines.

Mr. Smith received a Bachelor's of Science in Computer Science from the University of Maryland at College Park and a Master's of Science in Business from the Johns Hopkins University. He performed his doctoral work at Georgetown University in Washington, D.C., where he currently serves as an adjunct professor in the graduate school.

Mr. Smith serves as the Chief Information Officer for an organization based in the Washington D.C. area. He currently lives in Maryland with his wife.